THE NEXT TO LAST DRINK

THE NEXT TO LAST DRINK

Lois Mathieu

Acknowledgements

Thank you so much Beth Lynne Grace for being my faithful reader. Your careful eye and thoughtful commentary helped to make this story the one I wanted to tell. I am indebted to my late brother, Don, who schooled me on the complexity of addiction as he struggled to break the cycle of using alcohol as a remedy for anxiety. With thanks to my husband, Bill, for always listening.

Why do you stay in prison
when the door is so wide open?
- Rumi

DEDICATION

To Joyce and Judith, my beautiful sisters.

CHAPTER 1

Union Station

W ill Valentine drove around the busy corner of Union Station, feeling the twinge in his stomach that woke him at dawn. His dreaded appointment with Grace Manning wasn't until 10:00 a.m., and so there was enough time to stop at Newberry's for a carton of cigarettes. He had already smoked much of his last pack, and what was left of it would not get him through the rest of the day. It was time to quit the thirty-year habit. But this was not the day to anguish over another go-round of withdrawal from nicotine.

The morning sun reflected on an object in the vicinity of the variety store where he usually parked his car. Will soon recognized the beacon of light as yellow police tape glinting at the far end of the street. "Damn, of all times," he mumbled, thinking that if the trouble was more than a fender-bender it might involve Phineas. He decelerated the car to a near halt and considered leaving the area so as not to park off the beaten path. But he was concerned about Phineas, who was up in years, and so he turned down the dismal side

1

street and parked his old Volvo where the tall half-empty buildings kept out the morning sun.

Will turned off the motor and looked around. The only activity in the street was two plastic bags billowing up from the gutter, kite-like and mimicking transparent jellyfish guided by an invisible string. He got out of the car, feeling the stinging bite of air that made him regret not bringing the gloves his sister had given to him the previous Christmas, expensive leather gloves in his dresser drawer, still in the holiday box. But no one could have anticipated the detour that caused him to go off the beaten track. He zipped his leather jacket closer to his neck and then turned into the wall of wind tunneling down the sidewalk corridor with a strength rivaling gravity, forcing him to slow down. There was humor in it, Will thought, the way the wind was taking charge of his full body weight all the way to the open avenue.

A small crowd had gathered near Newberry's Variety, which Will noticed was clearly outside the boundary of the police tape. His eyes continued to water from the cold wind, and now he was eager to feel the warmth inside the store. He opened the door with more force than was needed, causing Phineas to look up from the counter, startled. In his late seventies, his well-boned face revealed the handsome boy inside. He was neatly attired, as was his custom, with a blue denim shirt and a dazzling multicolored tie.

"Will!" Phineas exclaimed.

His normally calm demeanor accelerated into high gear when he blurted out the news. "A man was shot this morning, right out front! Cops say it was drug related."

Phineas' store had been family-run for two generations, but now it bordered the notorious battle zone around Union Station. Never before had serious trouble come so close. He was visibly shaken and needed to talk about the incident.

"I was in the back," he related, "opening up some cartons, and I heard two shots. For a split second I thought it was a motorcycle backfiring, but there was something different about the sound and then I knew it was gunfire. To tell the truth, I was leery about coming up front. By the time I got the nerve to look out the door, it was over; a man was lying in the street and Gus was talking on his radio to headquarters."

"You mean a cop shot the guy?" Will asked.

"Yeah," Phineas replied, all worked up. "It was Rodriguez! You know, Gus. Seems the robber shot first and nicked Gus' shoulder, and then Gus fired back. I mean, it was a matter of life and death. The ambulance came and the attendants put the guy on the stretcher. He might have been dead. The attendants wouldn't say. Gus is a family man. It could have been him. It's getting to be too much with all the drugs on the street. You can't even live a normal life, always having to watch your back and lock up like you're in prison. One of these days, I'll be closing my business. I'm too old now to move to a new location."

Will shook his head. "I'd hate to see you have to close the store, but the street's not safe like it was in the old days."

"When my pop opened up, Union Station was a nice place," Phineas said, proudly. "Everybody knew everybody in those days."

"Yeah, your father wouldn't recognize the area now."

Will's appointment was pressing on him but he didn't want to rush off and leave his old friend in the wake of the disaster. He waited until Phineas was done with talking about the incident. When it seemed that he had gotten it fully off his chest, Will put money on the counter and motioned for his usual carton of Marlboros.

"Smoking is getting too expensive now and I hear the price will be going up again," Will proclaimed, changing the subject. "That should be reason enough to quit."

"It's goin' on ten years since I quit," Phineas boasted, slapping the carton on the counter, showing his usual feisty style. "Best thing I ever did," he said, handing over the change. "Thanks, Will . . . bag?"

"Nah, that's okay. Wish I could stay longer, but I have an appointment across town. Tough day, Phineas."

"Yep . . . you never know how close you are to being stopped dead in your tracks. I guess when you're time is up, it's up," he said, a tremor of fear still in his voice.

Will went to the door and both men nodded to say their good-byes.

There was plenty of time to make his appointment with Grace Manning. It was more the chill in the air that caused him to hasten to the car. The wind on the side street was still blowing furiously, though now it was pushing him from behind, a bold and determined force guiding him against his will. When he drew closer to his car he caught sight of a small book lying near the rear wheel on the driver's side. He tossed the carton of cigarettes over to the passenger seat before picking up the book. He looked around, half expecting someone to call out for it. But, the street was still empty, and he held the book in his hand, stupefied at the sudden realization that he couldn't in good conscience toss it back into the street. There was no choice but to take the book with him and figure out a way to find its owner at a later time. He turned on the motor then quickly skimmed through a few pages to see what the book contained, discovering that it was a personal diary. He had done nothing wrong yet he felt guilty after reading the first line: *My name is Faith, I'm an alcoholic.*

"What is this, a joke!" he said aloud over the synchronicity of events and the odds that such a diary would come into his hands on this day. He slid the book beneath the carton of cigarettes, as if it were contraband, then drove off in the direction of the old schoolhouse on Elm Street. He tried to make sense of the bizarre events that had fueled the anxiety he had been keeping at bay since 5:00 a.m. The crime in front of Phineas Newberry's store was troublesome enough; now he was in charge of a diary that didn't belong to him— and there was no telling where that would lead. Too much to mull over now, he thought, putting on the signal light for the left turn to Grace Manning's office. He knew little about the woman. Not that it mattered.

He slowed down when he saw the rust-colored brick building that once was his elementary school. His professional eye noticed the restoration work—pointed brick and new windows that made the old school attractive again. The clean lines of the building represented to him the best in architectural design where form followed function, a philosophy that challenged his creativity by imposing a sense of purpose to artistic rendering. Will watched a young man take the steps two at a time all the way up to the main entrance door, the way he used to. That was long ago and the memory of it had nearly escaped him.

A narrow driveway led him to a rear parking lot where he discovered a world of small businesses he never knew existed; he sat in the car long enough to open the carton of cigarettes and slip a fresh pack of Marlboros into his pocket. He hesitated a moment before getting out of the car, feeling the oddest sensation of being a stranger to himself and thinking, *this is it, you crazy bastard, you're as ready as you'll ever be.*

Inside the building, he heard people going up the stairs to the second floor, and their voices echoed through the main hall. The old school was busier than he had expected it to be, and the spirit of the place seemed palpable as he made his way down the corridor, passing each room in search of Grace Manning's office. The smell of wax on the wooden stairs brought back old memories of the school bell ringing and classmates rushing by in new leather shoes.

Will unzipped his jacket to allow for more breathing room. He slowed down when he approached the door that displayed the nameplate of Grace Manning, Ph.D., Licensed Clinical Psychologist. He held back, remembering it as the door to the principal's office. For a moment he considered turning back, his mind behaving like a toggle switch—*yes*, *no*, until he quit deliberating and opened the door. A quiet bell announced his presence in the small reception room that housed half a dozen chairs, a coat tree, and a magazine holder displaying information on mental health, and alcohol and drug addiction. The cold gray walls did no more than hold the room together. Will stood for a moment in deadening silence not wanting to remove his jacket.

His nerves tricked him into thinking that coming here was a mistake, and he vacillated before committing himself to the simple act of hanging his jacket on the coat rack. He looked at the literature in the magazine holder and noticed his reflection in the black Lucite. There was more silver in his hair than he had remembered seeing when brushing his teeth that morning. Will had allowed himself to believe that a little silver in his hair was from years of hard-drinking more than aging; as though earning it was better than being handed it. In his heart, he was still thirty-something, but, in fact, he was the father of a grown woman. Even so, he was still handsome as a movie star, and not even alcohol had dulled the brilliance of his deep blue eyes.

Will sensed that someone was in the inner room— Grace Manning, no doubt. His quirky nature made him want to bellow forth *your head case is here*, if only to break the tension. His dread of sitting face-to-face with a *real* therapist exacerbated the tension from the bizarre morning. He was familiar with *group*, as it was called in the recovery program, and surely that was less intimidating than a one-on-one therapy session. Will had put up with group because it was a given in the program, and at times he even thought it was helpful; but he often used a disparaging term for group when he was with his sister, Blair.

His throat tightened under the collar of his new denim shirt and he loosened his tie enough to ease his air supply. A cigarette was what he wanted; needed. The absurdity of the situation was in knowing that he could easily put an end to the misery by turning the doorknob and making a quick escape down the hall and out of the building. He sat there, estimating the time it would take to reach the parking lot.

But Will was no coward, and so he continued turning the pages of the dull magazine while keeping an eye on the door to the inner sanctum. First, he heard a click, and when the door opened Grace Manning stood before him. She was dressed in a charcoal woolen suit, her wide shoulders holding up a thick mass of peppery hair. A broad smile revealed the most beautiful teeth he had ever seen. Will was transfixed by her wide set eyes, amber eyes embedded with tiny nuggets of gold encircling the pupils. He was immediately taken in by her imposing face, a bronze sculpture that might have been from another continent; too magnificent to be taken in at once.

She extended her hand and spoke in a low-timbered voice. "I'm Grace Manning. You must be Will."

"Yes . . . nice to meet you," he replied, turning up his best smile while trying to regain a sense of balance.

Grace Manning invited Will into her small office where an unexpected hint of cinnamon made him think of pie on Thanksgiving, and his nostrils flared to take it in. A large black coffee table sat between two chairs, a dull brown club, and a yellow high-back reminiscent of a throne.

"Please have a seat," Grace Manning said, moving toward the yellow chair and directing Will with her hand to sit in the brown club. Now, the stranger was back in his shoes. He did what she asked and sat down, thinking, *so far so good, you crazy bastard.*

In moments, the initial commotion had turned quiet, and now Will was face to face with the woman. Any second, she would get the session underway and he would have to explain why he was there. He felt a strange disconnect to the man he was on the drive over; as though someone else had inhabited his skin, some crazy son-of-a-bitch who would have to admit to a woman that he could no longer hold his liquor. In a fit of sheer lunacy he expected her to inquire about his homework or ask him if he had ever lied to his mother, but he quickly regained his senses when Grace Manning asked, "Did you have any trouble finding the clinic?"

"No, no trouble at all," he replied, wondering why she had asked.

"Some people coming here for the first time find themselves in front of the *Small-Animal Clinic.*"

Will hadn't noticed the animal clinic when he arrived in the parking lot, but he took to the humor and they laughed as if they were long-time friends. For the first time that morning he drew an easy breath.

She means well, he realized, genuine the way she makes eye contact. *Eye contact always tells*, his mother had told him as far back as high school. Grace Manning put down a manila folder that bore his name, and Will was chagrined by the fact that a file had been prepared already by someone who knew little about him; that it had been entered, no doubt, into a goddamn computer file. Had he been thinking clearly, he would have known that, as a matter of course, there would be a file; there must be a file for Will Valentine. He would have to get hold of himself and stop interfering with the purpose of the visit.

He put on a smile, and once again he allowed himself to be fascinated by the majestic goddess sitting in the yellow chair that caught fire each time the blazing sun shot through the window. Relaxed now, he regarded Grace Manning's noble face; a queen, perhaps, from some exotic land. He was certain that the woman could readily make her boundaries known; not from anything she said, exactly, but by the way she said it.

Alas, the small-talk came to an end when Grace Manning placed her hands on her lap and asked Will about his family and his work.

"I've been divorced for a number of years," Will said, grudgingly, mistakenly thinking that this revelation might put an arrow in her quill for later. He was sensitive about his failed marriage and he didn't want to be raked over the coals by talking about it at length. He was a professional, a prominent architect with some eminence, and that's the man he wanted her to see sitting in the brown club. But, Grace Manning didn't batten onto his divorce and, instead, asked about his daughter. Will talked freely about Samantha, who lived in Michigan and had taken a job at the university after graduation.

"Samantha was twelve when the divorce was final, and I immediately became one of those weekend fathers. But we have remained very close, even though we only see each other a few times a year."

Will explained that his father had passed away and that his mother had sold the family house and moved into a condominium.

"My mother and sister live close by. My sister and I re-established our relationship a year ago, just before I got sober. Blair has been a good sounding board this past year and a good friend."

Will shifted in his seat, sensing that at any moment Grace Manning would ask what brought him to her office, and so he shortstopped her.

"I'm having a tough time with feeling nervous. I guess you'd call it anxiety. It's getting harder for me to stay sober."

"Can you say more about that?" Manning asked.

He was a man, after all; not expected to talk about his feelings, and so he reached hard for an answer. "I feel shaky inside . . . feel it in my chest. I've come close to drinking because of it. I need something more than AA meetings to get me through this period, maybe a medication for anxiety. Sometimes it's so bad I won't even go out to the store. It's hard for me to interact with people. I can handle not drinking but I can't bear the jittery feeling . . . makes me feel out of control."

There! He said it. For the first time in his life, he had admitted to someone other than Blair that he was nervous.

"In what way do you feel out of control?" she asked.

The rest was not easy for Will to put into words. "It's just that I can't function normally, you know, like not wanting to be with people or making plans or sitting through AA meetings." He described his feelings as best he could.

"Go on," she said, her eyes showing interest.

"AA's literature was helpful when I first started the program, but I've had my fill. I worked through *Alcoholics Anonymous* and *Twelve Steps and Twelve Traditions*, and *Living Sober*, and sure, I'd like to have met Bill Wilson."

"You're in the company of millions, Will. How are you doing with the twelve steps?"

Will pushed himself to be candid. "I can't say that I've truly processed the steps. I've kept sober all these months by will power mostly, and maybe some special luck. I still find it hard to accept that I'm powerless over alcohol. That's not easy for a man to admit. But I fear that my will power might run out, and then what. All those years when I drank, I wasn't aware of anxiety, probably because I was consuming vodka every day. Now that I'm sober, I feel anxiety rearing its ugly head. I don't know how much more of it I can take without resorting to alcohol. I really need some relief."

Will searched her eyes for a positive sign regarding medication, but when she offered none he pushed harder to make his plea. "I know medications are frowned on in AA, but where does that leave me? I need help *now*."

He wasn't used to asking for help, but in that moment he felt something give way, as a clutch releases before the train pulls out of the station.

Grace Manning affirmed what he already knew about using medications in the AA program. "We've found that people do better when they really work the AA program, step by step. Meetings are more important than you may realize. Recovery is not just keeping sober. It's transforming yourself so you can live your life without being on the knife's edge."

Her kindness was bringing him no closer to where he wanted to be.

"The journey toward recovery is different for everyone," she continued. "Some people make time to volunteer in the community, or they start a hobby, and some even return to school and get into a new line of work. There are endless ways to bring quality into your life."

Will listened politely to what he thought of as the Sunday school lesson. Little of what she said could be refuted. He struggled, trying to think of a way to render his plea while she embellished on the cold-turkey treatment for recovering alcoholics, what seemed to him like one size fits all.

"Medications can easily become a crutch, even those considered to be non-addictive. But, if we determine that medical intervention is necessary, we'll find a way to fit it into your program. I'd like to know more about the nature of your anxiety. A psychiatric evaluation would be helpful."

Well, dickhead, this is what you thought would happen!

Will grimaced, deliberately, wanting her to see his dismay.

She smiled and offered the quiet, reasonable logic he couldn't counter. "Don't be concerned about seeing a psychiatrist, Will. It involves little more than answering questions about how you relate to the world in which you live. Every therapist has been through it, including me. An evaluation will serve both of us. It will allow me to provide you with good therapy and also help you understand yourself. If it turns out that medication is warranted, we'll work out a plan for you to use it in conjunction with therapy."

The idea of seeing a psychiatrist didn't come as a surprise, but Will felt the noose tighten when Grace Manning offered to arrange the appointment right then. Again, she reassured him.

"Really, Will, this is a tool for both of us to help us understand your condition and determine the best way to treat it."

"You're right," he heard his voice say. "After what I've been through, I should be able to handle it."

The words hardly left his mouth when he felt that he had done himself in, as if someone else had been talking for him.

Grace Manning went over to her desk and phoned the psychiatrist's office.

"I'd like you to see Andrew Worthington. He specializes in addiction-related issues, and he's very good."

"Okay," Will said perfunctorily, knowing he could have backed out.

"Do you have a preference about the day or time?"

"Not really," he replied, and then somewhere in the distance his name was being given, and in the hazy confusion he heard Grace Manning address him again.

"He has an opening a week from Thursday at 10:00 a.m."

His eyes thought for a moment and then he nodded. "Okay."

His future was coming at him at warp speed, and there was no stopping it, no opportunity to backpedal out of all that was being put in place. By now, it was easier to go along with the plan, and besides, he liked Grace Manning—the way she was cool about psychiatry, treating it as if it was an ordinary experience for people like him, not just the crazies. His resolve had weakened, *maybe seeing a shrink isn't so bad.*

The sunlight on the yellow chair might have charmed Will and got him talking about his drinking *career*, as he called it. Grace Manning was curious about when it began. He was candid about his experiences in Alabama, yet he kept away from telling her about a few episodes he wasn't proud of; not because he thought she was naive about what men do when they drink, but he didn't want to be perceived as a man without conviction, a lowly drunk. They were both professionals, after all; he wanted her to see him as he saw himself and not as some guy from the street looking for drugs.

He was still talking when he sensed that Grace Manning was winding down the session and getting ready to schedule his next appointment. The time had passed quickly. They agreed to meet the following Tuesday.

"Before you leave, Will, I'd like to demonstrate a simple breathing exercise that might help you to relax." She opened her hands in front of her chest and abdomen. He watched and listened.

"When this area is tense, the whole body is tense, and when it's relaxed the whole body feels peaceful. The way to do this is to take in three or four breaths slowly and deeply, feeling the intake all the way down to the abdomen rather than stopping it at the chest. Exhale while keeping the stomach area extended and soft; not pulling in as you would for good posture. For some people, it's easier to do this lying down or sitting so your back is supported. You'll feel the muscles in your abdomen relax after a few breaths. Try it with me now just to get the hang of it."

He forced himself to demonstrate his proficiency. Suddenly he just wanted to get out of there. He was done.

"What's good about this exercise, Will, is that it can be used anytime. Remembering to do it is the key to its success. You'd be surprised at how many people simply forget to do it. Like any exercise, you should try to make it a routine. You might also look into basic Yoga exercises. Bookstores are full of information on Yoga techniques. If you'd like to discuss this, I'd be glad to devote a session to it."

He said nothing and nodded. *Just relieve my anxiety! I'll think about Yoga another time.* He was glad when she went on to something else. He knew next to nothing about Yoga and, for now, he wasn't interested in knowing more.

While Grace Manning busily collected various pamphlets for him to take home, Will's eyes were drawn to the wall behind the big yellow chair, to a painting of a woman in a cobalt blue dress; a mother sitting in a garden, sewing a white garment draped over her lap, a child sitting at her feet. He was struck by the woman's gaze, fully attentive to the child looking at a picture book, her cheeks like fruit falling forward by their own weight.

A wooden horse stood in the foreground of the painting, reminding Will of a toy horse he had received one Christmas, when he was a boy. He wanted to linger in the moment but his gaze was interrupted when Grace Manning brought forth the pamphlets she had selected. She was aware that his eyes had been fixed on the painting.

"That's a Monet print from the Museum of Fine Arts in Boston. It brings life to these barren walls. Now, Will, here's a pamphlet about the careful use of medications, and here's a little booklet that explains the basic Yoga exercises. Take these with you and next Tuesday we can go over any questions you might have."

So soon, it seemed, their session had ended. They walked to the door and shook hands as friends.

"Thanks, Dr. Manning."

"We'll be seeing a lot of each other, Will. Please call me Grace."

He retraced his steps down the hallway and used the side door to get out to the parking lot. He noticed the animal clinic across the way and wondered how anyone could actually pull up to it by mistake. It crossed his mind that Grace Manning had told him the story to break the ice. He didn't care because he liked her well enough whether it was true or not.

The cold air put a charge on his gait, and he was ready to light up. Maybe this would be his next to last carton of cigarettes, he thought, walking toward his car, remembering how he had used that mental trick after his relapse eight months ago. He had been at death's door, and even then, he couldn't bear the thought of the last drink because it signified the end of life as he knew it; instead, he waited until he could say my *next to last* drink. That gave him an emotional buffer, wiggle room for bracing up for the last drink.

Will put the cigarette to his lips and inhaled deeply. The barrier he had felt on the way into the old school building was no more. It had vanished in less than an hour, as though a fog had lifted and cleared the way for a clearer vision of what was in the wake and what was up ahead. For the present, he was centered in the quiet moment of feeling well about himself.

His trusty old Volvo agreed to start and he would head home with the friendly invitation to call his new therapist Grace. He glanced over at the near-forgotten diary he had placed on the passenger seat only an hour before. The book didn't belong to him, and he didn't want it in his possession.

Now, he regretted picking it up. *Why now, of all the god-damn days, did I have to find that book?*

Tired relief flowed through his body from the events of the day that had begun with the shooting near Newberry's Variety Store. It was funny the way it went with Grace

Manning, he thought, driving out onto the main street to go home. In one hour, he had revealed more about his past than he had ever related to anyone.

He made a right-hand turn, then turned left and slowed down as he drove passed Sonny's Place. When he was half a block away, Sonny's red neon sign trailed him in the rear-view mirror. Vodka crossed his mind, but the thought was gone in a flash. He was strengthened from his meeting with Grace Manning and pleased with himself for getting his message across that will power alone was no match for his anxiety.

He considered the activities Grace Manning had suggested for him and quickly rejected them out of hand. There were things he liked and things he didn't like . . . simple as that. He truly enjoyed his profession, and he would be first to admit to being well suited to architecture because it gave him the freedom to define and control space simply by the lines he created—a room here, a wall there, a door no one would open until he put it into existence. He believed that using his imagination to create something out of nothing was like the magician who pulls a rabbit out of a hat with surprise to everyone but the magician. Will assumed that those lines only existed on paper, failing to recognize that he had drawn lines for himself. He wasn't a follower and he refused to be pigeon-holed and so his self image was that of a man who had no walls and barriers. He was about to discover the self-imposed walls he had built and maintained that kept him from personal freedom and growth. The oddest aspect was that he wanted to be a free agent but, in fact, he was guarded to a fault.

Will thought about Yoga and meditation, but that was not in his interest; nor was he a churchgoer or a person with a hobby. He barely tolerated AA meetings and, above all, he hated the idea of seeing a shrink. But he was an honest man, and that enabled him to admit to himself: *what I like most is drinking, but I'm not about to tell her that.*

For now, he was sure of two things: medication was necessary, and relief had to come soon. He was counting on Grace Manning to provide both.

Turning into the driveway, Will felt the chill of perspiration under his arms. The warmth of the apartment couldn't come soon enough. He grabbed the carton of cigarettes and the diary and went up to the second floor. The aroma of Rosa's cooking told him that a hot meal was at his door. He opened the door to his apartment, balancing the hot dish. Church bells rang from half a mile away, and the crazy thought struck him that only wedding bells last, not the marriage. Now, after all the years of addiction, he had begun the long journey to unravel the events of his alcoholic life. He would make tea and save Rosa's meal for later.

CHAPTER 2

Moving to the South End

It was almost a year since Will had given notice to Frank Sasso and left the prominent architectural firm of Sasso & Fern. He had been an important player there and quitting the position required much deliberation on the part of Frank Sasso, until there was no choice but to let Will go. The handwriting was on the wall when Frank took him aside and all but begged Will to pull himself together. Months later, alcohol poisoning nearly cost Will his life and at that time he quit his job and got serious about his addiction. He looked for another apartment that would save him some money and put him in proximity of the clinic.

Frank put him in touch with the Chichettis, Chichi and Rosa, who owned a two-family house in the City's south end. To Will's happy surprise, the roomy second floor apartment came with Cozy, a little white dog with silky fur marked with black only on his ears and tail. Cozy was allowed to roam free between the first floor and the second floor, and he had learned to gain entrance to Will's apartment by paw-ing at the doorknob.

The well-kept house was in *little Italia* where people came from all over town to buy bread they couldn't get in any other part of the city. They'd cue up on weekends to buy Italian meats and imported cheese. Customers would sam-ple pieces of Provolone and close their eyes in delight as the saltiness hit their tongues. Zinno's was known to have the best Sopressata and mouth-watering olives. People talked about the old country while gazing at scenes of sunny Italy on wall posters that depicted tiled rooftops and villas with lush gardens overlooking the Mediterranean Sea.

This delightful neighborhood was where Chichi and Rosa rented out their tidy second floor apartment. They had no children but the little dog, Cozy, was their pride and joy. Chichi was an artisan by trade and he could carve just about anything out of wood. He also planted a vegetable garden each year but not before a priest, the nephew of Chichi's friend, Luigi, came to bless the soil for the new season. Chi-chi's prize was his fig tree. He cared for it like a baby waiting to be born, burying it in the ground every fall according to Italian tradition. Miraculously, the tree survived each win-ter and flourished again in the spring.

The day Will moved to the apartment, Chichi and Luigi paced back and forth in front of the house like two old un-cles, anxious to help Will move the cartons upstairs. Cozy followed after the men all afternoon. When the last carton was brought upstairs, Chichi called for Cozy, and it took some time before he was found curled up on Will's sofa.

Rosa had spent the afternoon preparing a gastronomical feast. The spicy aroma of garlic and herbs wafted up to the second floor and Will found himself wishing for a nice Italian girl to come home to. When the move was completed, Rosa invited Will downstairs to share in the meal. Cozy turned round and round with the excitement of seeing Will at the table and then settled down between Will's feet.

Will was introduced to Rosa's delectable fried zucchini and pasta with meat sauce. But the main course was served when she brought out roasted chicken with all the trimmings. Will got permission to sneak tidbits of chicken to Cozy, and from then on the two were inseparable.

The next morning, Will got a late start, having slept past seven. Chichi was outside waiting for him, anxious to show off his fig tree and the garden of newly planted tomatoes, eggplant, squash, and cucumbers. Chichi enjoyed telling Will about the neighborhood traditions and rivalries, that every year he would do his best to beat out Luigi, who currently held the record for growing the biggest squash in the south end; and that Luigi made a special wine from a blue grape no one else could find. "He won't say where he got the grape," Chichi said with a wry grin.

By nature, Chichi was spare as a sparrow, wizened not so much from age as from wear. To Rosa's chagrin, she couldn't put fat on him. A big-hearted, big-bodied woman, her size alone made her boss of the household. She had given Chichi the back of her hand more than once, which was why he took her demands seriously. Rosa spent much of her time in the kitchen and was known to command people to eat at her table. After Will moved in, it became routine that two or three times a week she'd send Chichi upstairs to leave a hot meal at Will's door.

The two men took a liking to each other. Will was always willing to give Chichi a hand in the garden and with heavy lifting. They spent many hours shooting the breeze in the work shed, and when Chichi discovered that Will knew something about machinery and tool-making, he regarded him as a father does a son.

The first time Chichi brought out a bottle of wine, Will explained that he couldn't drink alcohol. Immediately, Chichi understood about the wine. "I know, Will," he said. "I know about the drink. It's no good for you."

But, Will didn't turn down Chichi's hot peppers, expecting to be up for the challenge.

"Here's the pepper I told you about, Will."

Cicchi watched as Will bit off a small piece of pepper and immediately began coughing. Rosa brought over a glass of water and Will kept his tongue at the edge of the glass until the pain subsided. Cozy danced around the kitchen, fully appreciating their good time and laughter. And then it was Chichi's turn. He carefully regarded Will's face as he bit into the long skinny green devil. His face winced and his eyes watered, but the old man held his ground and he even went back for more. Except when he was playing cards with Luigi or hand carving a fine piece of cherry wood, this was the most fun he would have on a given day.

During the winter, Chichi spent many afternoons at the Italian Club a couple of blocks from his home where he would drink wine and play cards with Luigi, Giacco, and Sal. After reaching what he thought was a respectable level of inebriation, he'd walk home, sometimes more than a little stewed, and Rosa would sit him down and yell at him in Italian while serving him fried zucchini, black olives, and Italian bread.

In the summer, the men used the early morning hours to tend their gardens and sometimes when work was done they'd start a game of bocci ball and play until they ran out of steam. They all had wives who seemed to pay them no mind; to their consternation, the women always knew of their whereabouts, and so year 'round, when it was five o'clock, the men faced the music and went home.

When Chichi first brought Will over to the Italian Club he introduced him to Luigi Boccierrelli. Will shortened Luigi's name to Bocci Luigi and that made the men laugh. They were immediately drawn to Will's good nature and sense of humor, admiring him for playing everything close to the vest and never carrying one man's word over to another man's table. And so, Will enjoyed living in the south end and spending time with Chichi and his friends. He gave the aging men something to look forward to at a time in their lives when there was little left to remind them of their youth.

CHAPTER 3

Blair

Will woke up at 5:45 a.m. by a thumping sound of the newspaper being tossed up the stairs. He rolled over and breathed a long sigh. *Rosa*, he thought, *what a blessing!* When he opened the door to get the paper, Cozy was waiting for him. In a few moments his coffee was ready and he read the paper while sipping the brew. When he was through with the sports section, he looked over at the diary on the coffee table. The meeting with Grace the previous day had left him feeling out of sorts but *the damn diary* was another matter. The first entry made him feel as though he had intruded on someone's privacy; even worse, it made him uncomfortable about his own sobriety.

I admit I want to be sober but I can't say I want to give up drinking.
Something inside me is as frozen as a cemetery in winter, ice unable to thaw.
I close my eyes and imagine myself freely moving with a brook, overflowing,
reshaping. There is a long wait through all seasons, and I fear being frozen
again in winter. When the ice begins to melt I venture out on a conduit of

light that takes me far and beyond. I move on a small sliver of hope that goes past the farthest reaches of the circular structure of my mind and I try to approach the mystery. I turn back. My face flushes with fear and I quiver in the trenches of my skin knowing that one of these days I will have to turn myself in. I want to be sober but I can't say I want to give up drinking. I have the tiger by its tail.

This was not what Will wanted to read. It was time to place an ad in Lost & Found.

Will looked forward to seeing his sister in the afternoon. She'd want to know everything about Grace Manning. Blair was the career girl who had never married and remained devoted to her family and two genial cats, Castor and Pollux. Her esteemed position at *The Gazette* kept her commuting to Boston twice a week though she did much of her writing at home.

Blair was good at her job, the way she was with everything she had undertaken; in the previous year she had been chosen to cover political unrest in South America. There was David, the man she met while doing a story on the West Coast, but the distance between them had made it difficult for a relationship to get off the ground. They were not exactly starting out in life—he had a history and she had a career. Blair had always relished the freedom she had from being single and her good fortune of being able to travel on the spur of the moment; for the time being, life seemed next to perfect.

Will and Blair had taken different paths after college. She was the warrior sister who fought hard to resolve her brother's restless nature, certain that if he could believe in himself as much as she believed in him then his life would be easier. After seeing the hold alcohol had on him in the months that led to his sobriety she came to realize that the complexity of his problem went far deeper than she could have imagined.

Addiction was difficult for Blair to accept because it defied logic and was out of her control; and no amount of devotion to her brother could take away his desire for alcohol. She was the fixer who might have been swept into the maelstrom of Will's addiction had he not kept his drinking problems to himself. Now, she rode the fine line, bolstering his spirits and seeking the help of alternative remedies that lined the shelves of health stores. Today, they had much to report to each other.

Will parked his car in the driveway. Blair leaned over the outside banister waiting to greet him. Who but Blair, he realized, would have an interest in the ordinary details of his life or even care about how his meeting had gone with Grace Manning. The sun glanced off her long amber pony-tail and fair complexion inherited from their mother, Lydia Blair Valentine. Will always knew when something was going on with his sister by the way the light moved in and out of the facets of her eyes.

"Hi," she said, greeting him with a smile. "Your friends are waiting inside."

Castor and Pollux were posed like bookends when he came into the foyer. They were part of the welcoming team and would be ready to jump on his lap as soon as he made it available to them. Blair, bright spirited as usual, beckoned him into the kitchen. He removed the diary from his pocket and hung up his jacket.

"It's freezing!" he bellowed in jest. "Turn up the heat."

Blair heard his request but was more interested in her most recent find. "You'll never guess what I found at Quality Herbs."

Will played along. "Okay, doc, what have you got this week?"

"Passion Flower!" she announced.

They moved into the stream of sunlight on the kitchen counter and read the label. "Passion Flower doesn't sound like a calming remedy . . . you sure it's not meant to stir me up? I hope this is better than the last one you bought."

They threw harmless darts at each other while Blair brought the tea water to a boil, then they went into her small study where the old library table she brought over from her mother's house held a prominent position in front of the window. Blair had purchased a Persian rug with a bonus check earned one year, and the rich reds warmed the study. The wall of shelves still contained the books from her college days in Middlebury, Vermont.

"Let's sit!" she said.

They put their tea mugs on the table. The wicker chairs crackled as they settled into their seats. Blair had adjusted the thermostat and now Will was warming up.

"Whatcha got?" she asked, curious about the little book she'd been eyeing.

"I found this on a side street across from Newberry's."

Blair's brow drew tight. "Oh . . . . I read about the shooting. Were you at Newberry's yesterday?"

"Yeah, I got there right after it happened. Poor Phineas was upset. I felt bad for the guy. He's always so chipper, but the look on his face made me see a frightened old man. His wife died a few years ago. Anyone his age would need someone to talk to at the end of the day. I couldn't park on the main drag because of the police tape so I had to drive down one of those ugly side streets. I found this book when I returned to my car. I'm sure it wasn't there when I arrived because I would have noticed it when I got out on the driver's side. It looks grungy from the dirt but the inside pages are clean."

He handed Blair the book. "Just read a few lines to see what I mean. It's like nothing I've ever read."

Blair flipped through the pages. "Faith," she read. "No last name?"

"No. She only goes by Faith. Whoever she is, Faith is recovering from alcohol addiction. It's almost too personal to read. I feel guilty, like I'm sneaking around in her private life. It's a little disconcerting. One minute I wish I could find her and then I think—not just yet, not till I finish reading it. It's her journey but, in a way, it's mine, too."

Blair read the first few pages. "Boy, this is really something. It seems almost *too* coincidental, don't you think?"

Castor and Pollux took turns performing pirouettes against Will's legs, purring louder when he reached down and stroked their ears.

"Yeah, it's kind of eerie. When I first opened it I thought it was some kind of joke. I mean, there I was, on my way to my first therapy appointment to discuss my own goddamn issues and I find this! In some ways I'm sorry I picked it up. Like, who needs the aggravation? Now I have to hope some-one claims it from Lost & Found."

"It's so bizarre," Blair remarked, "and to think that if a man hadn't been shot you wouldn't have found it. Well, maybe you should just go with it and not worry about how it came into your hands."

She handed back the diary. Will wanted to say more.

"At the end of the first section she says 'I have the tiger by its tail' meaning she wants to be sober but she doesn't want to give up alcohol. That's the way I feel and yet I couldn't have admitted that if I hadn't read it. I've never ad-mitted that to anyone, not in all these months in recovery. It's like opening the floodgate. Having this damn book is like having a tiger by the tail. I can't toss it and maybe I shouldn't read it."

By now, Blair was more interested in hearing about Grace Manning.

"Well, I wouldn't be concerned about reading it. That would be like wasting something valuable. If I were you, I'd read it. Maybe she'll claim it if you run the Ad and then the mystery will be solved. Maybe you'll find her at an AA meeting."

"Yeah, I'll have to listen carefully for the name, Faith."

"So, how's it going with Dr. Manning?" Blair asked.

Will described the old building and the stream of people coming in and out.

"No kidding, you wouldn't believe how much activity there is inside that old school. By the time I reached the door to Manning's office my heart was pounding. I don't know what I was afraid of, but I almost turned back. Lucky I didn't."

"What's she like?"

Will described Grace Manning as best he could. "Well, bottom line, I like her. She's hard to describe. I mean, you can't put your finger on her background. She's a mix. Her face is like a sculpture, makes you think of bronze. She's big, as in strong, not fat. She has this grand presence and she sits in this big yellow chair that looks like a throne. No kidding, it was worth the visit just to see her. She's like a goddess.

"She's probably late forties or fifty but that's hard to figure these days. She has these unforgettable eyes, deep amber with gold specks, like the eyes of the big cats in the wild. I've never seen eyes like that on a human.

"Yeah, she's really something. She talked a lot about medications and I told her about my past, you know, how it was when I started drinking. She made an appointment for me . . . to see a psychiatrist." Will paused for the reaction.

"You agreed to see a psychiatrist? What did I hear you say about a psychiatrist?" Blair exclaimed.

Will was prepared to qualify his previous stand.

"I know, I know," he said, laughing. "I said I'd never let a bad-ass shrink get into my head, but the way Dr. Manning presented the idea, well, I went along with it. Besides, I've been thinking that seeing a psychiatrist is the only way I can get a prescription for whatever it is I have. To be honest, I'm not thrilled about the appointment, but I'm not as against the idea as I was before. Dr. Worthington is his name. Ever hear of him?"

"No, can't say that I have. Hey, I'm just bustin' you about the psychiatrist. I'm glad you agreed to see him. So, when's the appointment?"

"A week from tomorrow. Good thing I don't have a longer wait. I could change my mind. Dr. Manning doesn't prescribe, so I have to see him to get on medication."

"Well, she sure moved quickly."

"She has a nice easy manner, but at the same time you can tell she wouldn't take any bull from anyone. You'd like her," he said.

They waited for Passion Flower to show some effect just as they had with Kava root a few weeks before. Blair asked, "Don't you feel any different?"

"No, I can't say that I do. Maybe it needs more time."

It might have been the experience with Grace Manning the previous day that put Will in a story-telling mood. Blair's cozy study provided an ideal setting for Will to talk about events in his life that she knew nothing about. All these years, she had viewed him through the prism of their childhood, and Will wanted her to see him not simply as the brother she knew.

Blair was curious about Sonny's Place.

"When did you start going there?" she asked.

Will thought a moment and recalled that it was more than twenty-five years ago. When he moved forward in his seat and propped up his elbows on his knees, Blair knew she was in for a long tale. "It was Ritchie who got me to go. You remember Ritchie. He came to Dad's funeral. He's the one who brought me to the hospital that night I nearly checked out."

"Yeah," she recalled, "the one with the straw-colored hair?"

"Yep, that's Ritchie," Will remarked. "Anyway, I was back from Alabama, just discharged. I didn't know much about the local bars, and I never went to any particular one. One bar was just as good as another. Ritchie kept twisting my arm to go to Sonny's Place to see this guy they called 'the Bear.' Seems the guy had been intimidating the clientele. You know . . . . a real asshole, the way Ritchie described him. He said the guy would get friendly but only after he had done you in, you know, like making you back off on some nonsense he put out. No one dared go up against him and he was taking over the place just by bullying. I guess Sonny was waiting it out, hoping the guy would just go off to another bar."

"A local guy?" Blair asked.

"No," Will said. "He came into town one day and just never left. Only later did I find out he had been a boxing champion in the Marines. When I met him, he weighed about two hundred and fifty pounds. No kidding! But, anyway, Ritchie finally talked me into going to Sonny's. He picked me up after work.

"Sonny's Place had a kind of saloon door entrance . . . still does for that matter."

"Like in the wild west," Blair quipped.

"Yeah, only Sonny's Place wasn't really all that wild. When we came inside, the juke box was playing one of those whining country songs and I remember the smoke curling up over the bar. I didn't look left or right, just kept walking behind Ritchie. I heard a couple of regulars saying *hey* to Ritchie as we walked to the end of the bar, down near the men's room."

Blair listened hard as Will continued with his story.

"You never knew Ritchie, but he could make me laugh harder than anyone. For some reason, the Bear never fooled with him. Ritchie was over six feet tall and he had some flesh on his bones, and I think his happy-go-lucky nature could fool you into thinking he was never serious about anything. There was this flop of hair always sideswiping his forehead . . . and he had a habit of running it back with his hand as if to clear his view.

"I'm getting sidetracked. So, I put down a ten to cover the beers we ordered. There was something about the quiet that made me think the Bear was in the place and then Ritchie gave me a sign to let me know the Bear was sitting at the other end of the bar. I decided to wait awhile before turning my head to get a glimpse of him in the mirror that ran the length of the bar."

"That meant you had already walked by him on the way in!" Blair exclaimed.

"Yeah!" Will replied. "All of a sudden, the Bear got up off his stool and headed right for us. That's when I felt my adrenaline kick in. But he walked right by and continued on into the men's room. Poor Sonny looked over at us and just raised his eyebrows. I didn't know him at the time, and I even wondered if he was a coward by putting up with the guy so long. If it had been my place, that guy would have been out on his ear already. Anyway, this was my initiation to Sonny's Place.

"So, Ritchie and I waited. Then we heard the toilet flush. We looked at each other, expecting the Bear to walk on by because we had heard the men's room door open and then close. We sat still, looking straight ahead. Sonny was about to come our way with the beers. Suddenly the Bear reached out and snatched my ten-dollar bill from the counter, right before my eyes. I turned around and locked eyes with him. No shit, he looked meaner than the guys I knew in Alabama, but I was charged up and ready to take on the son-of-a-bitch.

"Omigosh, what did you do?" Blair asked. By now, she was fired up.

"I said, 'Hey, that's my ten bucks you took.'

"The Bear said, 'Yeah, and how are you going to get it back, ma boy?'

"That's when I squared off, thinking *you fucker, those eyes don't scare me.* I could see what Ritchie had been talking about. This is how the guy would intimidate customers just coming in for a beer.

"He was built for battle, like he could stare you down without even looking at you."

Blair laughed, her eyes indicating that she wanted to hear more.

"Now I'm looking at the black hair coming up from under his tee shirt. No kidding, his back must have been covered with it. He had this small ponytail at the base of his skull that would make you think of a tail sticking out from the underbrush."

"Omigosh," Blair repeated. "He sounds disgusting."

"His enormous frame took up the space of two grown men. He looked straight at me and said something like 'chicken.' I was all ready to take him after he referred to me as *ma boy*. I mean, those are fighting words, but saying *chicken* pushed me over the top, and I wasn't even drinking. I can still hear that damn song playing on the jukebox, *you knocked me out with your love, babe, and I keep comin' back for more.*

"I think Ritchie knew history was about to be made when I looked the guy in the eyes and said, 'chicken?'"

The pupils of Blair's eyes widened as Will described the huge bear paws that gripped him around his arms, raised him up like a small child and flung him against a bar stool with a force that could have broken his back, but Will quickly stood up and he came at the Bear feeling a surge of strength he had experienced the first time in Alabama, and then it happened . . . . in a flash. Will's left hook shot up without warning and leveled the Bear, breaking his nose as well as a bone in Will's hand.

Will now shifted in the wicker chair as he described to Blair the sound of cracking bones and the pain that shot through his shattered hand, making him an instant hero.

"You mean the Bear hit the floor?" she asked.

"Hard as hell! It was worth a broken hand to see the son-of-a-bitch lying there with blood gushing from his nose. The guys who were there that night never forgot it. And, Ritchie never tired of telling the story and singing the juke-box song that played throughout the event."

Will heaved a sigh as if he had just been through the ordeal. "Sonny's Place became the hottest bar in town," he told her. "Even Sonny admitted that. Guys came from all over hoping to see some action, but they found out it was a mistake to fool with me. Every now and then, some guy would try to make a name for himself and I'd have to put him in his place. I'd tell 'em right out, 'Don't fool with me.'"

"It always comes to that in bars," Blair remarked.

"Well, that's what guys do when they're young and strong and ready to fight. It's hard to keep away from fights if you go to bars. Even a good bar will have trouble now and then. It goes with the territory. I soon found out that alcohol releases the control switch in our brains. Some guys get too feisty and too big for their britches. More than once I had to prove myself just because I had a reputation and some fool wanted to challenge it."

"God, what a vicious cycle," Blair remarked. "But what happened to the Bear after that?"

Will laughed. We became . . . friends, kind of. You know."

She shook her head. "The ways of men are sometimes difficult to comprehend."

"The thing is," Will told her, "he never came back to Sonny's. I'd see him once in a while in another bar. The last time I saw him was about eight years ago. He got fat and sloppy. Who knows where he is now. He was one of those guys who would keep coming at you like a steamroller unless you had the courage to hit him right between the eyes. You wouldn't understand that," he said, seeing the look on her face.

Warm tea and storytelling put Will's anxiety on hold for most of his visit that afternoon. It was after three o'clock when he was ready to leave. He stood up and looked at the colorful book covers embracing the room. Will pointed to a book about heroes of the century. "Heroes," he said. "Wouldn't you think one of them would know something about anxiety?"

"Only artists can tell us about such things," she said.

"Speaking of artists," he said taking down a book on the Impressionists, "I saw a Monet print in Manning's office." He thumbed through the pages.

"Here it is. Look. This reminds me of a small wooden horse I had when we were kids."

"I love that painting. Yeah, the horse looks familiar."

"Tea's cold," he said. "I guess that means it's time to go. I'll be stopping at Mom's. She needs me to change a light bulb in that ceiling light she can't reach. If the sun lasts, I might even drive down Laurel Road."

The intensity of daylight was beginning to fade by the time Will got into his car. Blair called out to him from the front door. "Hope you find the owner of the diary," she said. "Phone me after your appointment Thursday. Say 'hi' to Mom!"

Will nodded *yes* to everything she was saying, then waved and drove off.

There was just enough sunlight left to make the drive to Wintonbury worthwhile. Will hadn't seen the old neighborhood in months. Turning down Laurel Road he remembered that it was a dirt road until he entered fifth grade. That was the year he came home with a still-life charcoal drawing his teacher said revealed extraordinary artistic talent, and upon her recommendation he was sent to art school for a three-week summer course. After the first week, Will told his mother that he wanted to quit so he could play softball with his friends; but she talked him into sticking it out to the end. She was the disciplinarian in the family, making sure her children brought home good grades and that they finished their assigned chores at home. As far as Lydia Valentine knew, her children did what was expected both at home and at school.

Will peered from the windshield hoping to get a clear view of the brook that ran parallel to Laurel Road and flowed all the way to the cemetery where it collected into a small pond. Kids in the old neighborhood ice-skated on that pond and they played baseball on the open land awaiting new graves. He remembered the sweltering days of summer when they'd cup their hands under the faucets and slurp

the cool water down their dry throats. Mike the caretaker guarded the cemetery like a hawk. As new graves were
needed, the pick-up teams shifted the bases, and by the time
Will was in ninth grade no space was left and baseball in the
cemetery had ended for good.

The cemetery had been a kind of sanctuary. It was
where Blair and her best friend, Cara, had smoked their
first cigarettes. They rolled them up using a rusty old de-
vice Will had found in the cellar. He chuckled now at the
thought of teaching her how to dry the corn silk and using
it as tobacco. The trick, as he recalled, was to bring just
enough saliva to the tip of the tongue, then quickly seal the
thin sheet around the corn silk. *Like smokin' pot*, he thought
now.

"Sit under the tree on top of the vault," he told her. "No
one will see you there." Kids in the neighborhood knew it
was where dead people were kept when the ground was too
frozen to be dug. Only boys would walk past the vault after dark, but on a summer afternoon anyone would be safe
sitting on its grassy rooftop in the shade of a large maple
tree. In his mind's eye, Will could see Blair walking down
the road with a pitcher of grape Kool-Aid, and Cara carrying the peanut butter crackers and the cigarettes they'd hid-
den someplace. It was just the two of them, setting out for
their first smoke, needing no one else in the world. Blair
told him later that they hadn't expected to feel such a harsh
bite from the sweet corn silk. They withstood the pain until they couldn't take it anymore and then came home. He

laughed now thinking of how brothers do things like that to their sisters.

He drove slowly past the mailbox the owners had put up for number 253 to identify the two-story clapboard house set way back from the road. A tricycle turned over on its side flagged his attention, and Will resisted the urge to drive up the long driveway and check to see if the old swing still hung from the backyard pine. A tan pick-up truck was parked further up into the yard where Will learned to drive his father's car before he was twelve-years old. Hugh Valentine's machine shop couldn't be seen from the road, and Will wondered what it was being used for now.

Lydia Valentine had sold the family homestead that included several acres of land, and from what Will could see, it was being well tended. The house and barn across the way were in need of repair, and, as Will now recalled, they were always in need of repair. The original owners, all dead now, had raised chickens and pigs and kept a few milking cows and a couple of plow horses. The pigs were mean. Every day, they chased Will on his way to school until he learned how to turn and stare them down to scare them off. Blair never forgave those neighbors for slaughtering pigs in the backyard. Will told her not to watch, but she indulged herself anyway and came home with pig's blood on her forehead.

Those days began with the incredible sound of roosters; and everywhere, cows and sheep grazed in the meadows. Life moved along without any notice of itself, and from what Will could remember, neighbors were generally quiet and unassuming, as if no one had much to complain about. Will now drove by an old farmhouse overlooking the rolling acres he knew so well, imagining that the ash-colored sheep were those he had seen every day on his walk to school; always skittish, moving and darting in a wave as though directed by the slightest current of wind. *Still rural*, he thought about Wintonbury, *but different*. Dusk settled over the meadow as unobtrusively as a soft blanket, making it difficult to see much beyond the road. Will continued on to his mother's condo several miles away.

CHAPTER 4

White Lightening

William's second appointment with Grace Manning got off to a good start. She was interested in what made him decide to join the Army and he explained that after completing two years of college at the state university his funds were getting low and he didn't want to put further burden on his parents.

"I could have worked and gone to school part time, but I decided to let the Army pay for the remaining courses. Besides, I was glad to leave Connecticut and strike out on my own. As I think back, that might have been my motivating factor."

Grace wanted to know more about his experience with alcohol when he was in the Army, and he was better prepared to talk about it on this visit.

"I probably would have started drinking even if I didn't join the Army. At first, the smell of beer sickened me. It really made my stomach turn. There was this guy . . . Red was his name, who could drink three beers in an hour and that impressed me in those days. Hard to believe now that drinking a whole bottle of beer was an important goal. More than once, I had to rush off to the men's room to release what my stomach knew to reject. I should have given it up right then and there. Anyway, by the time basic training was over I was pretty used to alcohol. Also, I was gaining a reputation for my left hook that I didn't know I had it until I joined the Army. After basic, I was sent to Edward Gary Air Force Base in Texas to train as an airplane mechanic. I'm not sure if, being a woman, you can appreciate how I felt arriving there feeling fit as a boxer . . . ready for the next round."

Grace understood very well what that had meant to him, having counseled men of various backgrounds and experiences. "It sounds like every weekend you were the new colt breaking out of the starting gate."

"That's exactly how it was. I became a small celebrity to the guys after they saw my fighting skills, and that sure made weekends more exciting."

"You were in a different element with those country boys from the south."

"As a matter of fact, it was more like being in another country. I remember how some guys would argue about whether Texas was in the south or in the west. I didn't care where it was located, only that it was sure different from up north. They were *mean bastards* with their segregation laws."

"What do you remember about that?" she asked.

"I got my eyes opened going into town on the weekends and seeing for the first time white bars and colored bars, white restrooms and colored restrooms, all those awful bigoted signs ruining everything. I was used to playing ball with everybody and going to school with everyone all mixed together. We all sat in the same classrooms and used the same bathrooms and even my neighborhood was a bit mixed. Of course that makes it sound like happy family. I'm sure if you asked any person of color how it was growing up in the north the story would be quite different. It's just that down south the separation was so . . . so vulgar, claiming segregation as a natural law, and boy they were ready to defend it. Awful. But maybe the only difference was in the signs, whether they were actually posted or just taken for granted. Desegregating the Army did more for the cause than anything because it was on a grand scale. It sent a big social message across all cultures that couldn't be ignored.

"There was a guy, Toomey. We were friends. Toomey got me into a colored nightclub to see *The Platters*. After so many years it seems like yesterday . . . Toomey coming over to my bunk and asking me if I liked *The Platters*. Who didn't like *The Platters*? He told me he could get me in if I didn't mind going to an all-colored club. Imagine! Toomey had a good sense of humor. He said, 'Now, don't go trying to get me into one of your clubs.' I remember telling him that I didn't know of a nightclub he couldn't get in until I got past the Mason-Dixon Line. I'm not sure he believed me."

Will recalled how Toomey could tell a good law from a bad law just by sniffin' it. "'Like smellin' fish,' he said. 'You know it right off.'"

Grace chuckled.

"I believe you told me last time that you went to Alabama after Texas. That must have been another eye-opening experience for a northerner."

"What I remember most about it was how ugly it was, at least where I was located. There was this guy in the barracks from North Carolina. We called him Clay because he was always complaining about the red clay in Huntsville. No kidding, that place was all clay and all ugly. Clay called me *white lightening* because of my fist. He knew how to make moonshine. One day he asked me if I ever drank the stuff and I told him I'd heard about moonshine but never even saw it. He warned me—not to drink *white lightening* unless I knew how to test it. I can still hear him with his country accent explaining the whole process.

"'Y'all go up in the woods, way up, and you make it pretty fast. Y'all don't go too long distillin' it. Gotta work fast. When the money guys come, y'check the bead. Y'tell good corn by the bubbles . . . . how long they last. Some light it first . . . . see if it burns blue. Best way I know is checkin' the bubbles. But, don't fool with it. Don't drink the stuff with anyone you don't know. Ya'll go blind. White lightin'll kill ya.'

"When I left Alabama, I never saw Clay again. Now I realize I almost forgot him."

For a split second, Grace's smile was much like his mother's smile when she had listened to the full account of his day at school.

"What did the men do on weekends if they didn't drink?" Grace asked with a quizzical look.

Will shook his head in dismay.

"They were flat out of luck. Drinking in the Army was expected, and gambling and fighting often accompanied it. I guess that's what men do when they're young and full of whatever it is that makes them always ready for action—testosterone I suppose. If you can't be one of those guys, you're out of the loop. There were some pretty hard fistfights. I was born with a fist like a weapon, and I discovered that my left hook could put a guy on the floor. No one could see it coming. Red, the beer-drinker, always kidded me about it. 'Hey, Will,' he'd say in front of the guys in the barracks, show us that fist of yours.' And, I'd say, 'sure, you'll see it when you least expect it,' and they'd laugh."

Will kept in mind that Grace did not share his experiences, and he held back from telling her about his less noble escapades when he was out with Red, which, even to this day, he regretted. Instead, he focused on the fistfights.

"Driving home from a bar one weekend, Red asked me if I ever thought of going into the ring and I told him I'd only fight to defend myself, not for sport; you know, with all the activity that goes on in bars there's bound to be a fight. I remember him saying, 'Hell, the only worthwhile activity in Huntsville takes place in a bar!'"

It was clear that alcohol had put Will in the comfort zone. Now, in telling his story to Grace, he could see that alcohol had also fueled a desire to fight, which, until that moment, he had maintained was for self defense. By now, Grace had heard enough about drinking and fighting. Will's candid account had given her a snapshot history: a man with many valences, an innocent who started out in rural Wintonbury and worked himself both in and out of hell from alcohol addiction. The goal now was to stay out of the self-made prison. The session was just about over. Will could have said more, but there would be time for that. The important thing was that he liked the bronze goddess in the big yellow chair, who listened to him with the interest of a mother who could just as well sit him on her lap and tend to his wounds.

CHAPTER 5

Bocci Luigi

Will was comfortable living in the apartment upstairs from Chichi and Rosa, and by the time he started seeing Grace Manning, he had been there for nearly a year. In the summer, he worked with Chichi in the garden, breathing in sweet honeysuckle. He'd rub the tomato leaves with his fingertips and experience the unique aroma that brought him back to summers growing up on Laurel Street in rural Wintonbury.

Chichi told stories about the days when he was a boy, arriving in America with his family from Calabria, Italy. His first memory, he told Will, was one of excitement and feeling at home in the neighborhood because there were so many Italian immigrants beginning new lives in America. He remembered the sparsely settled neighborhood.

"Not like it is now with everything so built up."

Some of the men owned tractors. In the spring, they turned over the soil so people could get their land ready for the planting season. Much of the produce grown on small farms got sold to markets. Wives stayed home and minded the children but they weren't afraid to put their hands in the soil. Many of the immigrants were artisans and tradesmen. Chichi was skilled in woodcarving. The south end quickly became the place to find all sorts of specialties in food, stone and hand carved tables. People shared a common goal of owning a home, and in a few years some of them earned enough money to buy property to rent out. Chichi spoke with pride when he talked about his parents' generation, recalling how hard they worked from dawn to dusk. "A lot of work, a little Provolone and homemade wine," he said. "That's what makes life sweet."

On a Saturday morning, Will packed up the trunk of his car with fishing gear and a cooler of beer, and then drove a couple of blocks to the Italian Club where Chichi and Bocci Luigi were engaged in a game of cards. Will came inside, hearing their laughter. Bocci Luigi had been putting the heat on Chichi, saying that his trousers were too big.

"I justafasay, Chichi. She gotta feed you more. You gonna starve to death."

The men laughed.

"Hey, what's so funny?" Will broke in.

Bocci Luigi let him in on their friendly banter.

"Chichi's wife. She don't feed him so good. Look! His pants are falling down."

"Come on, Will, sit down," Chichi said. "Don't listen to Luigi, he don't know what he's talkin' about."

Will had something adventurous in mind that he couldn't wait to share with the men. "What do you say we go fishing at Beaver Lake?"

As if on cue, they looked at the clock on the wall.

"Don't worry," Will said, allaying their fears. "I'll have you home by five."

Will left the two men, who by then were showing signs of ecstasy, and he walked to the corner market for bread, cheese and Capracole. When he returned to the Italian Club, the card game was over and a bottle of homemade wine was on the table. Off they went. The grown men were gleeful as children, happy to be going out with Will and given to laughter because their wives didn't know where they were going.

The threesome hauled their provisions down to the gray wooden dock at the edge of Beaver Lake. Will gave the dockhand a couple of bucks to rent the row boat, and they rowed out to the place where they were told the fishing would be good. To Will's surprise, Bocci Luigi knew more about fishing than he did or Chichi.

The men told stories while they drank wine and ate sandwiches, and when the wine was gone, they drank the cold beer from the cooler. Will kept sober with a couple of bottles of ginger ale, but the men drank heartily.

The sun was hot, the air cool and breezy. They had a few nibbles, but there was a long time between bites and nothing stayed on the hook. Will figured that their voices might have caused the fish to go away. But, no one cared because they were all having too good a time doing what they hadn't done in years. By late afternoon, Chichi and Bocci Luigi were feeling mellow from food, wine, beer and sun.

When it was getting on to five o'clock and time to call it a day, Chichi suddenly felt his line jerk.

"He's a big one!" Chichi yelled.

Bocci Luigi called out with his furry voice, "Chichi, you got em!"

To their dismay, the line had been snagged by the floating branch they had been avoiding all afternoon. Chichi tried in vain to disengage it but the line wouldn't give way.

When they were about to give up Will had an idea. "Wait!" he said. "I'll swim out and free up the line. I just need something to slip under it and raise it so I can pull it off the branch."

Chichi unfastened his belt from his trousers. "Here, Will, use it to lift the line."

Will switched seats with Bocci Luigi who was now the faithful navigator. "Okay, Luigi, you're in charge," he said.

Will took the belt and swam out toward the branch. It took a few tries to slip the belt under the line that was caught on a nodule. Will manipulated the belt outward and upward until it was in position to lift the line.

"Steady, steady, Will," the old man kept yelling. Will lifted the belt one more time and the snagged line released from the nodule, and he struggled to keep the line free long enough for Chichi to regain control of it with his fishing rod.

"We gottim, Will! We got the son of a bitch!" Chichi called out with delight.

Meanwhile, Bocci Luigi kept the boat nosed in the right direction, making it easier for the old man to maneuver his line. Chichi's face beamed with anticipation. He felt the fish tugging on his line, the weight of the fish pulling the line taut. Will kept his eye on Chichi's line to be sure that it maintained a distance from the branch and then he swam back to the boat. By then, the old man was struggling to pull in the big catch of the day while trying to keep his trousers from falling down.

"Chichi," Will called out when he reached the boat, "keep reeling it in!"

In an instant the big catch was flipping in front of Chichi's face. The older men were like two proud boys as they gazed at the large brown trout, guessing that it weighed about nine pounds. Will hoisted himself into the boat. They all laughed with gusto as they rowed to shore, each in turn recalling who did what and when. The dockhand awaiting them helped the older men get a footing upon leaving the boat. When on firm ground, Chichi asked for his belt, but Will didn't have it.

"I must have let it go out there," he said to Chichi. Now they had even more to laugh at when they recalled that Chichi's baggy trousers had been the topic of discussion earlier that morning. Chichi had to admit that his trousers were in fact too big, roomy enough to slip down. But this was a day without care, and so he was happy enough to pinch them together with one hand until they reached the car. Will opened the trunk and put their prize in the cooler. They drove home, laughing to beat the band, with Chichi and Bocci Luigi mellow from wine and grateful to Will for their big adventure.

Will dropped off Bocci Luigi at his home and then drove around the corner to Chichi's house. It was already six o'clock. Suddenly, all laughter ceased. Rosa was pacing out front. She stood with her hands turned backward on her hips, the way she did whenever she was about to chastise the old man in Italian.

"I justafasay," Chichi said to Will with a wry smile and feeling a little tipsy, "she's a big one!"

"You get out and I'll go to the trunk for the cooler," Will advised with a hint of sympathy in his voice.

Chichi stepped out of the car, still pinching his trousers, and Will went to the trunk. Rosa started in on the old man right away. Instinctively, both men avoided making eye contact with her. In Italian, Rosa asked Chichi where he had been all afternoon and why he was so late.

Chichi sported a guarded grin. "Will took me for a ride."

He held his trousers tight and looked at Will who was now hoisting the cooler out of the trunk. Rosa continued to chide Chichi in Italian, accusing him of never coming home with anything but an empty stomach. Will placed the cooler on the ground, and Chichi relished the moment of presenting Rosa with the freshest fish she had ever seen. As she continued talking with her hands, Chichi let go of the pinch on his trousers just long enough to open the lid of the cooler.

"Guarda!" he said, looking down at the fish as his trousers fell to his knees.

The startled woman didn't know which to look at first, the large brown trout in the cooler or Chichi's exposed male member. Will moved hastily to help Chichi pull up his trousers while Rosa stood there with her hands covering her face. The woman was shocked, speechless for the first time in her life, yet her eyes sported a glint of amusement. Without blinking, Chichi secured his trousers with one hand and grabbed the cooler handle with the other. Will assisted him and together they carried the cooler down the sidewalk to the backyard and placed it on the step.

Cozy came along wagging his tail and he sniffed when he got close to the cooler.

"Okay," Chichi said to Will, winking and waving him off. "Go upstairs. Take Cozy with you."

Will left the scene in great haste, figuring there was nothing more to be done for the old man that day.

CHAPTER 6

Buffalo Boy

Wednesday seemed endless. Will moved perfunctorily from one errand to another in anticipation of seeing Dr. Worthington the next day. There was just so much he could do to take his mind off the appointment. He thought about Phineas and what he might be going through since the shooting, which the newspaper had reported to have been fatal. He would check on Phineas before taking his shirts to Laundry Express and stopping at Burger King.

The police tape was gone. The neighborhood appeared to be back to normal. *A man was killed and everything looks the same*, Will thought, parking in his usual spot. He could see Phineas standing behind the counter as he approached the door. A bell had been affixed to the door and it caught Will by surprise when he opened it.

"Phineas, how's it going?"

"Hey, Will. Better than the last time you were here. It took awhile for things to settle down. 'Course, the neighborhood will be talkin' about it for a long time. I guess you read that the shooting was fatal. Gus won't be over this one for a long time. How about some coffee? I just made it."

"Sure," Will said, pulling up a stool.

"It's been quiet here today," Phineas remarked, handing Will the coffee. "I've been meaning to ask how your mother is doing."

"My mother is fine. She takes a walk most days and keeps herself trim. She still looks youthful for a woman her age. I saw her yesterday and she was telling me how her father let her drive in the city when she was only fourteen years old."

"Yep. You could do that then," Phineas remarked. "Glad to hear she's making it okay on her own."

"Yeah, she has a couple of widowed friends living in that complex. They keep busy. She wasn't one to fold up after losing my dad. I'm glad for that. She likes it when I stay for supper. We talk about the old neighborhood but mostly she enjoys talking about the days when she was growing up and how she met my father. I drove by the house yesterday afternoon, so I was able to give her a full report. When the cold eases up, I'll take her for a ride so she can see it for herself. She's happy knowing that the property is being kept up and that a family with kids lives there."

"Your dad had the best machine shop around. I guess you weren't interested in machine repair and tool making," Phineas remarked.

"Not really. I worked for him when I was in high school. He said I was good at it . . . well, at least he never complained about my work. He could take a piece of metal and make just about anything out of it. But, I just couldn't see myself doing that for the rest of my life. He wasn't one to venture out, just happy to have his shop on the property with my mother nearby. He'd help out during the planting season and then my mother would take over until late August when it was canning time and then he'd pitch in again. They were well suited. He never said much when I started at the university but I knew he wanted me to stay and work in the shop. Yeah, he liked having everything just so. Good thing he had my mother."

"That's the way it was then," Phineas said. "Not like it is today. Times have changed, that's for sure. I don't know if that's good or bad."

"I have to admit," Will remarked, laughing, "it's easier when someone does your laundry. Speaking of laundry, I'm on my way to Laundry Express."

Will put the cup on the counter. "Thanks for the coffee, Phineas. You always make a good brew."

As evening approached, Will tried not to think about his meeting with Dr. Worthington. It was a mistake, he thought, not to have picked up a film. News and sports were what he usually watched but tonight he needed something more engaging than what the program guide listed. At seven o'clock he gave in and drove to the video store. The mall was busy for a Wednesday night.

What is this? he wondered. *Kids should be doing their homework*, but, then, a school holiday would have escaped him. He watched parents and children making choices as if they were at a buffet brunch, picking from shelves that were neatly stocked with bang-bang-you're-dead flicks and adult themes smartly packaged for the whole family. Will walked away from New Releases and moved to the Adventure category where he found a flick called *Buffalo Boy*. The blurb read: *An orphaned boy out West is raised by a wise recluse after the Gold Rush days.*

He came home and brought the water to a boil and swished two tea bags back and forth until the color was deep amber, then set the mug down and pressed *play*.

Buffalo Boy was what he was looking for.

The story, set out west in the late 1800s, told about men who had finished their last dig after being swept up by the Gold Rush. Chou Li, who had come from Guangdong Province in southern China, had dug up enough nuggets of gold to claim one-hundred acres of land.

Now, years after his rush for gold, Chou Li remains vigilant. Not a day goes by that he can let down his guard because of bandits who roam the territory looking for gold that might have been left behind. He keeps his distance from the scattering of farmers in the sparsely inhabited land and rides a makeshift wagon into town every other week to replenish supplies and sell parts of the buffalo he kills. No part of the buffalo goes to waste, and he skillfully dresses the meat, preserves the hide and pulverizes the bones.

Only a small herd of buffalo roam the land, but Chou Li remembers when they moved in a body as large as a country all the way to the Canadian Territory. Chou Li is naturally skilled to live off the land, never trying to outsmart nature, instinctively knowing when to put down the pistol and when to pick it up. He's built spare with a fixed smile, charcoal eyes, and long spatulate thumbs he uses as tools.

For most of his life Chou Li lives with the asceticism of a monk from an ancient land. His hand-built cabin overlooks a fast running stream that provides him with fish and an occasional bath. The land behind his cabin sweeps up to a lofty knoll that overlooks his one hundred acres. A lone tree shelters one side of his cabin and spreads its spare limbs above a small wooden bench where Chou Li rests at the end of each day. He reads from a small book that was given to him by a wise elder upon leaving his homeland. The wisdom of the book keeps him on his true path that will take him back to his eternal home in the spirit world.

Chou Li takes down a buffalo with one shot, and then works the whole day dressing and carving the beast with knife and thumbs. He keeps an adequate supply of meat for himself and puts together the larger portion to sell on his next trip into town. Nothing is wasted, neither hide nor mineral rich bones. When his work is done, Chou Li sits under the tree and reads the sacred Chinese words from the worn pages of the small book. To Chou Li, the tree is also sacred.

By the 1870s, a much older Chou Li rides into town to get supplies and sell buffalo meat. On his way back, he follows a smoke trail in the sky all the way to the edge of his land where he sees the burned out cabin of a neighboring farmer. A few buffalo roam in the distance and a baby's cry gets picked up by the wind. Chou Li pitches his ear toward a moving stream and spies a baby sitting under a tree and looking back at the ruined cabin where his parents have been killed by marauders. Chou Li takes the child into his arms and brings him home. He calls the child Buffalo Boy.

Chou Li tells the boy he is his second father, and in time, Buffalo Boy addresses him as Second Father. Buffalo Boy is quick to learn from Chou Li. During the day they work hard and do little talking. Buffalo Boy does much watching and listening. Nature is their companion. There is a kindness in the old man as he teaches the boy to whittle wood. Master and novice, they share many enjoyable hours together.

When the time is right, Chou Li sits the boy down under the sacred tree and begins teaching him lessons from the small book. The words are memorized, but still the old man appears to read from the book. He teaches the boy that he will find wisdom from his relationship with nature and the universe, and that elders have wisdom that youth do not have. He tells him that the eternal presence provides a conduit for wisdom, and is a blessing and gift from the eternal soul.

He tells the boy that he will learn life's lessons from experience and that the wisdom in the book will help him find his right path; that following it will keep him strong. When the time comes for Buffalo Boy to commit himself to his true path, Chou Li speaks to him as the boy picks up a new piece of wood and begins to carve it in the shape of a small horse.

Chou Li tells him that they will someday walk the same path in the spirit world. The young boy's eyes grow big and black in anticipation. His small hand sweeps back his hair, rippling the sun through its blackness.

"We will ride our horses together in the spirit world, won't we, Second Father?"

Chou Li teaches Buffalo Boy that the time is coming for him to find his true path and that he must follow it until he draws his last breath. He tells him that he must learn to be the overseer of his own mind just as diligently as they tend the land together. He must not allow his thoughts to lead him off the good path toward destruction.

"Take charge of your mind. Never let wild notions roam untended in that big territory; otherwise they will grow like weeds and clutter your path."

Buffalo Boy asks with a little fear in his voice, "But, Second Father, how will I know if I am on the right path?"

Chou Li answers, "Soon, your true path will become known and you will no longer feel like a child or see like a child. You will begin to see things that need tending. If you ignore these things, your path will become overgrown and disappear before your eyes. Eventually, you may lose your way."

"Can I ever get it back again?" Buffalo Boy asks.

"Yes," the old man answers, "but it takes much hard work to retrieve it. If you abandon your path, you may be lost forever; then we will never meet each other again in the spirit world."

"If I lose my path, I know you will come and find me," Buffalo Boy says with confidence.

"I tell you what I know that was handed to me from the wise ones," Chou Li admonishes. "I only give you my blessing to carry in your heart and help you in time of need. Remember, in this world you must walk your own path to find truth. No one can walk your path for you and you cannot walk the path of another."

Buffalo Boy's eyes come alive with the revelation, as Chou Li continues talking. "Know your inclinations, for they will be with you all the days of your life."

The boy asks, "Do I have inclinations, Second Father?"

Chou Li says, "Everyone has inclinations. They are all the things you do even when you say you mean to do something else, like starting on a new piece of wood before finishing the last piece."

Aware of himself, the boy glances up and away, glad to see Second Father smiling at the inclination they both recognize.

"Inclinations are imprinted on you by your ancestors," Chou Li reveals. "When they reach you, they belong to you and you are responsible for them. Do not let them roam unattended in your mind; otherwise, they'll overtake you. Only let truth roam free in your mind. When you understand this lesson, Buffalo Boy, you will be on the right path."

In earnest, Buffalo Boy promises, "I'll never let my inclinations overtake me, Second Father."

Buffalo Boy goes everywhere with Chou Li and in time he gets to know every inch of the hundred acres. He stays close to the old man when they go into town for supplies.

There, people are attracted to the boy, and the old man is respected for having taken him in.

Down from the meeting hall, the Last Saloon continues to initiate youth to the ways of men with its dance hall, whiskey and gambling. Here, they fight off hard feelings with their fists when whiskey doesn't take care of them first. Chou Li knows the danger of whiskey and cards and tells the boy the saloon is not for him.

In time, Buffalo Boy is old enough to go into town alone to get supplies and sell his wares. At eighteen, he's handsome. People turn to look at his blue-black hair as he rides into town. He tips his hat and seems a cut above the ordinary cowboy.

One day he gets waylaid by Pete, a whiskey-drinking gambler, who invites him into the saloon. Soon, the young boy is sitting at a table with Pete and drinking watered down whiskey.

Pete tells him, "This is what *men* do."

Buffalo boy won't let on that he hates the taste of whiskey. This is the first time he's alone with someone other than Second Father and while he's more than a little afraid of Pete, he likes having a new friendship.

When Buffalo Boy returns to the cabin, Chou Li surmises where he's been; though says nothing about it. The next few nights, they sit together by the fire whittling wood in silence. Chou Li displays no anger, and they speak to each other in a cooler manner until it's time to go into town for more supplies.

A day comes when Buffalo Boy can't ride into town fast enough to pick up supplies, and he goes looking for Pete. The two men drink and play cards until late at night. Buffalo Boy slumps in his chair, drunk. When he awakens in an upstairs room he feels the morning air billowing through lacy curtains. An unfamiliar scent makes him feel a stranger to himself. He uses water from a basin and splashes his face to regain his senses. In moments, he's riding back to Chou Li, as if chased by the early morning sun rising fast on his heels.

Every other week, Buffalo Boy follows the same routine, and in a few months he's drinking like a man and gambling away more than he owns.

One night after much whiskey and gambling, Pete asks Buffalo Boy about his debt. "The land will be yours someday, won't it?"

"Sure," Buffalo Boy answers.

Pete intimates that the old man is probably going to die soon and suggests a way that Buffalo Boy can pay off his debt without Chou Li's knowledge. He tells Buffalo Boy, "You can pay off your debt an acre at a time. I'll wait until the old man dies to collect it."

The idea comes as a great relief to Buffalo Boy. Now he can continue playing cards and Second Father will not be the wiser. Together, the two men draw up a map and every couple of months they mark off the acreage that is owed Pete.

In a few years Chou Li is ready to die. He places his hand on Buffalo Boy's head and gives him his blessing. He closes his eyes believing that he leaves the boy with one hundred acres of land he has tended all these years. By this time, the map in the saloon shows that all but ten acres belong to Pete.

Buffalo Boy makes a coffin and digs Second Father's grave on the knoll overlooking the stream that sustained them both. He lays the small limbed body in the wooden box as he would a bundle of firewood, and guides the coffin down into the grave on a long piece of wood. Throwing down the first dirt, he realizes what he has lost and he begins to weep. For days, he weeps over the grave of the man who gave him a second chance at life.

When the weeping stops, Buffalo Boy comes out of his trance and gazes across the landscape, seeing with new eyes. He stops under the tree where Chou Li had taught him his lessons. There, he finds the small book Chou Li had left for him, along with the finished wooden horse that Buffalo Boy had started many years before.

Buffalo Boy carefully turns the pages searching for meaning in the Chinese characters he cannot read. He looks to the sky and realizes he will have to remember everything Chou Li taught him from the book. His black hair weaves in the wind and he breathes in the spirit of Second Father.

CHAPTER 7

Dr. Worthington

When *Buffalo Boy* ended, Will read for a while from Faith's diary. Much of what she wrote had escaped his understanding but the movie had put him in a different frame of mind; now he was feeling her words rather than intellectualizing them, absorbing them instead of grappling with them as objects.

> *The brook has never been this frozen. Nothing can budge until something begins the thaw. A frozen mind takes comfort in its own inactivity. The thought of venturing out keeps me shut down, a clam closed off to the outside. Blue ice has kept me a prisoner far too long. In my late winter dream, the sun gazes on the water and I sense the warmth. I break free and make my way to the surface. There, I view myself from high ground. Free now, my mind sees more than it wants to see. I must find the courage to withstand the thaw and live with pieces breaking off from my rusted out circuitry.*

He fell asleep with the book in his hand, and a dream took shape. He was a moving river, showing off as he rushed through a narrow winding groove over stones of blue ice embedded in the river bottom. He felt himself leaping with fish into the sun-lipped air. An old Chinese man appeared out of nowhere with his fishing gear and left a small wooden horse on the riverbank. The horse waited for the old man all afternoon, pretending to be real. Will witnessed the old man's fishing skills and he saw fish leaping into his arms. The sun followed the Chinese man wherever he walked and brought light to the river bottom where his feet walked on turquoise stones. Something floated to the surface. He searched for a basin. A hawk flew above the river and dove for food. The old man called out Will's name.

The diary fell to the floor and Will woke up with images of the river and a wooden horse on the river bank. He was too sleepy to discern whether the images were from the dream or the film, or from what he had read in the diary. He turned off the light and in moments he was asleep.

Thursday morning came, as he dreaded it would. He poured coffee and propped up the newspaper behind his mug where the reflection of sunshine struck the newspaper with such intensity that the paper might well have ignited the kitchen table. He glanced at front-page headlines and checked the sports page before turning to the Lost & Found section where he read his ad for Faith's diary. *What do I want?* He asked himself. He was aware of his indecisiveness, vacil-lating over whether he did or did not want the diary. Ini-tially, he wanted no part of it, then he wanted to read only a portion of it, and then he hoped no one would claim it, at least not until he had finished reading it. But Faith was opening him up to new vistas he never knew existed. He had been touched by art; not his kind of art, where the lines he drew defined the open spaces and gave form to emptiness, but Faith's art of venturing out onto the thin ice of fear and making it on sheer courage and faith.

Now he had to admit that Faith was no longer an intruder in his life. He wanted to know the identity of the woman whose writing about the trappings of life had touched him deeply and made him dream that he was a river. No one had ever touched that deepest part of him, not even himself.

I want to be sober but I can't say that I want to give up drinking. He kept this in his mind while driving to his appointment and he wondered if he'd ever be able to admit to anyone but Blair that Faith's words resonated with him so much.

Will arrived at Dr. Worthington's office promptly at ten o'clock and was greeted by a chipper receptionist who asked him to complete the usual paper work. Marcie was the name printed on her lapel badge. The thickness of the woman's body had obscured her youth, but she seemed happy in her skin, and Will thought her flaccid face to be pleasant, the sound of her voice soothing, feeling it right down to his groin, the way it happens sometimes hearing women's voices. He imagined that she had been one of those pretty high school girls whose heifer brown eyes and maternal breasts might have led boys out of puberty faster than they could say Jack Robinson.

She offered Will some coffee.

"No thanks," he said.

A few minutes later, Marcie announced, "Dr. Worthington will see you now."

Only then did Will figure out that there must have been a private exit for patients, as he had seen no one come through the waiting room. In one way, and out the other, he thought, and that pleased him.

Andrew Worthington stood up tall when Will entered the room; he came forward from behind his desk and greeted Will with a firm handshake. "Have a seat, Will," he said, posturing to the three chairs situated at a coffee table. Will sat across from Worthington, and with one chair empty he wanted to ask if they were waiting for Elijah but that would have started him off on the wrong foot. The casual arrangement was well-intended, he thought; allowing two grown men to suspend the unevenness of their relationship long enough to conduct an exchange that would leave them spent, one from spilling his guts, and the other from doing half a morning's work. Worthington opened up the dialogue.

"Grace Manning tells me you're in recovery."

Will gave him the short form about the events of the past year, explaining that anxiety was his reason for being there. He was aware that his presentation was stilted from trying so hard to give Worthington the impression that he was someone other than a bozo looking for drugs. They conversed about the trials of living day to day with anxiety with Will doing most of talking and Worthington nodding at intervals as might be expected. Much of what Will said was a repeat of what he had told Grace Manning. When only half the time was used up, Will became distracted by the mundane, perceiving that Worthington was in his mid forties and that his receding hairline might have begun at a young age. The session seemed to be going flat.

Worthington shifted the conversation and tried to get Will to talk about his early years. Will made an effort to cooperate but couldn't recall anything significant about growing up in Wintonbury, not one childhood experience that could be traced to his feeling of unrest. Worthington continued poking around in Will's family life as if he were looking for a needle in the haystack until Will cut him off at the pass.

"I find it difficult to talk about my personal life, my parents in particular. I mean, not so much in normal conversation, but like this. It feels unnatural."

"Males in particular are not used to talking about their feelings," Worthington said, as if this was news to Will. "Men are expected to get on with their lives without rehashing it. It's not easy for anyone to reveal their personal lives, particularly to a stranger. It may seem that I'm fishing for information but my intention is to bring your life into focus and help you find the source of your unrest."

Will nodded, acknowledging the reasonableness of Worthington's argument though not expecting to go further with the topic. Worthington crossed one leg over the other and linked his hands around his knee, as though preparing to dig further into the trenches. "It can be useful to bring old feelings to the surface. People easily get bogged down in life; yet, with a little reflection, they can relieve their desperation. In your case, you may have had feelings of anxiety way back."

Now what? Will thought, dreading the next thirty minutes.

But Worthington persevered long enough to break the icy barrier of Will's resistance by asking where he was stationed in the Army.

Will admitted that he had wanted to leave Connecticut and see other places. "Unfortunately, I didn't get any farther than Texas." They both laughed and that gave them the impetus to move forward, steadily, like water flowing again. Will told him that alcohol had been a remedy for anxiety when he was in the Army. He recalled that he had been restless as a child, and Worthington asked about those early childhood memories.

"I guess I assumed that what I felt was the way everybody felt. There was no history to go by or means of comparison. All I know is that when I started drinking in the Army, I felt relaxed socially. I was at ease with other people and with myself."

Worthington embellished on Will's insight. "It doesn't take long for the brain to record the experience of feeling better. That's where desire comes in. The mind remembers the better feeling and that fuels the addiction process."

Much of what Worthington told Will reinforced what he had gleaned from discussions with Grace Manning— that his brain was clever in its demand for alcohol. He gave Worthington a candid evaluation of his experience. "My brain signaled the desire for alcohol even when my body was being poisoned by it. It's a vicious cycle, but had I known about the danger of addiction twenty-five years ago, I think I would have continued drinking alcohol because it was readily available and a sure remedy for easing anxiety. I didn't know then that I had anxiety, but I sure as hell knew when I didn't have it. Nervousness, restlessness, whatever you call it, those were terms no one talked about in those days. Being a man, I just got on with life, and I got on with it by using alcohol."

Will paused a moment before asking, "What can I do now that alcohol doesn't work for me anymore?"

Worthington reached for his tie, as if it needed fixing. "One thing you know: Alcohol is not the answer. I'd like to see you a couple of more times even as you continue working with Dr. Manning."

Will nodded, though he was certain that there would be no further sessions unless he was given a prescription for anxiety. He listened to Worthington with guarded anticipation.

"I think you already know, Will, that alcohol can kill you if you keep using it."

"Yes, I know that, but anxiety is as much of a threat to me as alcohol."

"Anxiety can be dealt with," Worthington offered. "If we can get it under control, you'll be in a better position to benefit from therapy and build a life without alcohol."

Will nodded, wondering what he meant by getting it under control. He would ask flat out for medication, but first he threw out his last pitch.

"I need something that will help me sit through the AA meetings. Sometimes I feel so nervous I just . . . you know, up and leave. Dr. Manning wants me to participate in group therapy. I'm already anxious just knowing it's coming up in the future."

Worthington kept on about living one day at a time. "The best way to live life one day at a time, Will, is to remember not to venture out too far from where you are right now. I know this is easier said than done, but just think about it. If you spend each moment worrying about something that may happen in the future, or if you get lost in ruminating over the past, you'll lose out on the moment you're in, which is the only real thing you have. Some people worry so much that they end up not living in the present at all. It's like giving your life away. Life is to be lived and it is best lived in the present."

"I hear what you're saying. Alcoholics are good at living in the present particularly when we're drinking. We need to learn how to live that way when were sober."

"That's the goal. So, I'm not suggesting that you never think ahead, only that you spend your energy on what's important now. So, for example, when Dr. Manning says she thinks you should join the group, say yes or no when the time arrives but don't worry about it now. Hang on to your power. Don't spend it all on worrying."

Will couldn't but agree with Worthington. He nodded and then pressed him with the big question. "What about medication?"

Immediately, he felt like a man waiting out a sentence.

Worthington came through, finally, and said, "You're suffering from moderate to severe anxiety and some depression. I believe medication is warranted in your case."

Medication is warranted! Will repeated this to himself, hoping Worthington couldn't detect the joy in his face. Worthington used the remaining time to talk about the medication, and then he wound down the session.

It was over, finally. Will left with a prescription in hand and an appointment for the next visit. He walked to his car trying to shake off the lingering feeling of being someone other than Will Valentine. Worthington was a nice enough guy, he thought, but he wouldn't want to spend much time with him; and even being there for one session made him feel that he had gone over to the other side. But he got what he came for, and that made the experience of seeing a psychiatrist worthwhile.

The weather had turned cold and visibility was poor driving home. Christmas lights blinked on and off through the frozen windshield giving the impression that there was more activity in the street than there was. Much had been said in fifty minutes, and Will was emotionally drained. Ice continued to form on the windshield, even with the defroster on high. By the time he got home Will's eyes were strained from squinting and trying to see. He started up the stairs, and before he reached the second floor, his olfactory system told him that a hot meal was at his door. He turned on the TV when he got inside his apartment and immediately sat down to eat Rosa's hot Italian sausage and pasta. It was almost noon. Scientists were discussing dark matter in space, theorizing that black holes, previously thought to be nothing, are, in fact, filled with matter. *No such thing as nothing,* they conjectured. The notion was intriguing to Will, and he thought about the constellations he had learned in his eighth grade science class and wondered whether he could still locate Orion the Hunter and Draco the Dragon.

At two o'clock Will couldn't remember whether he was to phone Blair or she was to phone him. The package containing his new medication was on the kitchen table, still unopened, and for some reason he didn't feel compelled to open it. He went to the phone and stood for awhile, poised like a pointer, hardly sensing the passage of time. He decided to read the diary instead of calling Blair.

He thumbed through pages and reread an entry about the old fisherman who reminded him of Chou Li, the character in the video he had seen the previous night. Faith's words continued to connect with something buried deep inside him, liberating something the way sap can be teased out of wood. She had written about *the thaw* and *the rusted out circuitry* and he imagined being embedded in ice and wondered what it would be like to go through the thaw. *Would I find a gem at the bottom of it all?* Things float to the surface, Faith wrote. It would not be easy dealing with his rusted out circuitry from years of addiction. It seemed to Will that Faith was far ahead of him in the recovery process. He closed his eyes. *Take it slow with Worthington and Manning. Control the anxiety.* He fell asleep with the image of Faith stepping out of the water.

CHAPTER 8

Snow in April

It was not the first time Will had been awakened by the sound of the book hitting the floor, and he woke up with a start. Cozy was staring at him.

"Cozy, I didn't hear you come in."

The dog jumped up onto the sofa, stood on Will's chest and licked his face until he laughed and wrestled the dog into his arms. "What would I do without you, Cozy?"

The session with Worthington had tired him out, and much of their exchange was still resonating with him.

"Life is to be lived," Worthington had said, "and it is best lived in the present." Those few words were easier said than done. Faith's diary had comforted him but often the meaning of her words escaped him. *Water is flowing. When I step into the river I become the water and the prayer.*

The phone rang. It was Blair.

"I was waiting for you to call. How did it go?"

"It went okay," he reported. "I just woke up, must have dozed off. Well, bottom line," he said, "I have moderate to

severe anxiety and some depression. He prescribed a medication that has some promise."

"No kidding. I'm not surprised, are you?"

"Not really," he agreed. "I knew I needed something. I
thought the medication was just for depression, but I guess
he knows what he's doing."

"Did he mention side effects?"

"He didn't say much about that. My biggest concern
is that it could take up to six weeks for the medication to
kick in. I'm not happy about that. But at least I've taken
action."

"So, when do you see him again?" she pressed.

"He wants to see me for a couple of sessions and then
occasionally to monitor the medication. He said to call in
between if I need to talk."

"I feel like a weight has lifted." Blair remarked. "This is
good news. Did you sleep last night?"

"Pretty well . . . woke up twice but got back. I picked
up a film to take my mind off the appointment. That tells
you how desperate I was. But, it was pretty good . . . called
Buffalo Boy and it kept my mind occupied."

"I heard that you saw Mom Tuesday night?"

"Yeah," he said. "I stayed for supper."

"She told me. That made her happy."

"I wasn't hungry that early but I ate anyway and gave
her a full report on the old neighborhood. House looks good.
The people are keeping it up nicely."

"I'll drive by someday," Blair replied. "Hey, feel like
Scrabble?"

Will was tired, but he needed to unwind. "Sure, if the sleet stops. What time?"

"Come around six. I'll make something easy for supper. The sleet will stop from what I hear, and then the temperature will rise, and then get bitter cold. Sounds like New England, right?"

"Yeah, right about now I'm hankering for Arizona!"

Will hung up the phone and sat for a few minutes in the kitchen staring at the unopened package from the pharmacy. Cozy watched with interest as Will opened it, expecting a treat.

"Well, Cozy, here goes," he said, taking his first dose.

At 5:30 p.m. he put on a clean shirt, brought Cozy downstairs and then left for Blair's. The sleet had stopped and the sky was clear when he drove into her driveway. They'd been playing Scrabble together for months. The game helped sharpen his mind, which had been dulled by alcohol, and it gave them something to focus on while they caught up on the years when they hadn't seen much of each other. There was a time when he thought Blair was preachy because she had occasionally offered unsolicited advice about his alcohol consumption. She was two years older, and that had set the pattern for a lifetime. Except for his mother, she was the only person who could question him directly and draw out an answer. Once, he told her, "I don't want anyone trying to get inside my head or preach to me. My life is my business and I don't care to discuss it with anyone."

He knew at the time that Blair wasn't sure if he was giving her fair warning or if it was just an off-the-cuff remark, but she was wise enough to know that she belonged in some parts of his life and not in others. For the present, they were both glad that they had re-established their relationship and deepened their friendship.

Will rang her doorbell and gazed up at the stars trying to identify one constellation.

Blair opened the door. "Look at this, no more sleet. The sky is beautiful!"

Will came into the foyer and hung up his jacket. "Boy, something smells good."

"It's the potatoes roasting in the oven," she replied. "Nice shirt."

The table was set and the Scrabble board was out.

"We're having steak. I knew the sleet would stop and we could use the grill."

During dinner Will filled her in on the session with Dr. Worthington.

"Dressing's just right," he said.

They played two games of Scrabble while eating ice cream with hot fudge sauce and drinking nearly a pot of decaf.

"Since I stopped drinking I really crave chocolate. And I drink more coffee now than I ever did. They say that if the coffee machines broke down, the AA meetings would have to be canceled."

"If you ever start dating," Blair remarked, "you'll have to find someone who loves chocolate and coffee as much as you do."

"I wouldn't know what to do on a date," he said, laughing. "Do people still date? I was under the impression they just hopped into bed."

"Well, they don't date the way we used to, that's for sure," she replied.

"Did I ever tell you about the woman who came into Sonny's Place one night?"

Blair gave him a quirky look, anticipating that she was about to hear something about his darker side. "Are you sure you want to tell me this story?"

"Okay, Castor, you can come up now. See? Even Castor wants to hear this one."

"This happened years ago, after the divorce when I was drinking all the time. Anyway, she was nice looking, probably in her thirties," he said. "She used to hang out there occasionally. She came in when Sonny was about to close up and asked if a guy had been in looking for her. Sonny knew her type. He knew she was up to something. I was too drunk to care about what she was up to, but not too drunk to string her along.

"Anyway, Sonny asked her what kind of car the guy was driving and I think she said it was a blue Pontiac convertible. He just shook his head no. So, I put in my two cents and told her I thought I had seen a blue convertible parked out in front about an hour before."

"Was that true?"

"No," Will said, "of course it wasn't true."

"I would have thought she was in trouble and looking for a safe place to land. How did you know she wasn't in trouble?"

"She wasn't in trouble," he said. "She was *looking* for trouble. Hey, this is my story. Do you want to hear it or not? I was drunk. She was drunk, and Sonny and I knew there was no guy planning on meeting her."

"Okay, I get it."

"Some people are lonely, you know. She was looking for a guy."

"And you were the guy."

"Yeah, I was it. She came over and sat next to me and started talking, you know, all friendly like.

"I was so far gone. I thought I was stringing her along, but, instead, she was making the moves on me. She was drunk but not as drunk as I was. I told her I didn't think her friend was coming back and I offered to buy her a drink. We sat there talking and drinking, both of us skunked, while Sonny finished up for the night."

"You and the blond bomb shell!" Blair remarked.

"Well, blond enough," he said, trying to be funny. "Yeah, I remember a red dress but not much more."

Blair feigned disgust. "I guess a blond in a red dress is all that's necessary. You guys!"

"Anyway, she asked if I'd like to have some Wild Turkey at her place."

Blair was intrigued.

"She offered to drive. Her car was parked out front. In my condition, I couldn't have driven anyplace but home. She said she'd drive me back to my car in the morning."

"Do you remember her name?"

"No. When you're in that state of mind names don't matter. She drove me to her house. Well, I don't know for sure whose house it was, but it was one big son-of-a bitch in the outskirts of town. I couldn't find it now if my life depended on it."

"You mean a perfect stranger just took you home?" Blair was not goody-two-shoes but she couldn't imagine her own brother engaging in such conduct. "You know, men have it easy. They can do this sort of thing and get away with it. If a woman were to go off with a perfect stranger to *his* place she'd probably be killed."

Will laughed. "What are you talking about? What's the difference whose house it is?"

"Well . . . the difference is in who's doing the asking. If a man asks a woman to his place, she'll probably wake up dead." They both laughed at her logic. "What I mean is that if a woman asks a man to her place, he doesn't have to worry."

"That's what you think. You don't know the rules of the road as well as you think you do. Well, anyway, that's the way it goes sometimes in bars."

"So . . . what did you do, stay the night?"

"Longer. We drank Wild Turkey and other stuff, too. We were drunk all the time. She phoned some restaurant for food at night and somebody delivered the meals. I can't remember what the hell we ate, except I do remember eating potato skins for the first time and picking them up with my fingers. There was some kind of melted cheese on top and bacon. That was when restaurants around here were just starting to serve them. She wouldn't take any money, not that I had much to give her. We fooled around when the mood struck us, and we played cards, but we never stopped drinking except when we passed out. You know, we just did what people do when they're heads are screwed up. We never saw the light of day. The blinds were always closed and I never saw them open except once when I looked out the window and saw snow falling . . . like a veil in slow motion. It was Easter."

It sounds like a dream," Blair remarked. Will detected a bit of sadness in her voice. "What about ... well, never mind. I thought the woman said she would drive you back to Sonny's the next day. How the heck long did you stay?"

"More like a few days," he admitted.

"There's a lot I don't know about you, Will Valentine."

"You don't know the half of it," he admitted. "Anyway, she dropped me off in front of Sonny's on Easter Sunday and I never saw her again."

Will realized how incomprehensible this was to his sister, that he could behave in such a way even if he were shit-faced, which was the way he referred to his notorious binges. Will's drunkenness came as no surprise to Blair but waking up on Easter Sunday with a woman he didn't know was something that other people did, not her brother. Will detected a distressing look in her eyes, as though he had just now lost his innocence.

He left Blair's house well after midnight. The temperature had plummeted, but he didn't care because the week's events were over. By now, he liked Grace Manning, and he was even willing to put up with Dr. Worthington if it meant getting anxiety under control. The cold engine of his ten-year-old car started right off, and he thought of the previous winter when he drove out of the parking lot at Sasso & Fern for the last time. He had put the finishing touches on the drawings for Sweet's Convalescent Home and was driving over to Sonny's when he made the decision to quit his job. Only now did he realize how far he'd come since then.

CHAPTER 9

Group

Will's session with Grace was well underway when she brought up the subject of his divorce. Initially, they had glossed over the details. Will hadn't discussed the divorce much with anyone, always figuring it was water over the dam. Grace's question drew him out.

"You mentioned that your daughter was about twelve years old when you divorced. How did she handle it?"

Will shifted in his chair and thought hard before answering her question. "The way I remember it . . . Samantha couldn't understand why her mother and I had to live in separate places. I told her that I required some medical attention and that living alone would be better for me. That wasn't the truth but the explanation seemed easier for her to accept. She was happy knowing she could see me as often as she wanted. Fortunately, my ex didn't try to make things worse than they already were. She stayed close to my parents and that helped. Whenever there was a birthday party or holiday, we all got together. Barbara remarried when Samantha was in high school."

"How was that for your daughter?"

"Fortunately she was involved in her studies and sports. I think being busy helped. The guy didn't try to become her father and I think that made it easier for Samantha. He's the one who got her interested in applying to school in Michigan."

"It seems that you and your ex wife made an effort to handle the divorce the best way you could."

"Yeah, I guess. Our concern was always for Samantha. But, I don't care what anyone says . . . there's no good time for a couple to split after a child forms an attachment to parents."

"It's always difficult. How about you, Will? How did you fare after the divorce?"

"The marriage was over long before we legally split. Let's say it didn't come as any surprise to me when Barbara filed. She was pretty well worn out from trying to get me to stop drinking. I quit drinking for a while, but not long enough."

"What do you think is different about going into recovery this year?"

"A lot is different. The first time I stopped drinking, I didn't have a clue about how addicted I was. I always believed I could control everything with my will power. That's still in my craw, as you know. When I was younger, my body could take the hits, the beating up from so much alcohol.

But, when I got older, alcohol didn't give me the good feeling it did when I started out. I didn't want to believe that, and I tried every which way to continue drinking until I was just about looking over my own grave. One part of me admits to the addiction but there's that other part of me that wants to return to the bar, as if that's where I'll find the man I know as me. That's the part that needs to be dealt with. I have a lot more work to do. As far as addiction goes, I'm a lifer. My life has been shaped by addiction, and sometimes I think I may need another lifetime to find that person inside me who doesn't want alcohol; if one exists. I'm willing to commit myself to doing the work. What I'm mostly concerned about now is the anxiety. That adds another dimension that I never expected when I quit drinking. I may have had anxiety all my life without knowing it. Alcohol probably kept anxiety from gathering into a storm and unleashing out of control the way it feels now. I know one thing. Anxiety is not something I can control with will power."

Grace interjected. "You're among millions of people who use alcohol as a remedy for anxiety. So many people start out using alcohol when they're young, even before they know they're suffering from anxiety. When they start drinking, they feel better. As you know, it doesn't take long for the brain to start giving you feedback that alcohol is what makes you feel good. By the time it becomes a full-blown addiction, the vicious cycle is a trap for life. Both conditions need to be addressed. That's why recovery is so much harder work for people who are cross addicted to alcohol and drugs."

"Yeah," Will added, "I met some of them in the group sessions when I began my recovery last May. I don't know how they deal with that."

"They do better when they're supported by others who share that experience. In time, Will, I may ask you join a small group that meets here once a week. Your insurance allows for a certain amount of individual therapy sessions but *group* is what we do most of the time."

Group, now why did she have to go and say that?

He felt compelled to defend himself, even at the expense of sounding like a goddamn prima donna. "I really don't like the idea of being in a group."

"What is it about it you don't like?" she asked.

"It's just that . . . getting into other people's lives isn't my thing. I'd be uncomfortable talking about myself with people I don't know. Now that I'm off booze, I get nervous being with too many people. That's one of the difficulties I have with AA meetings. I rarely stay to the end. Sometimes it's because of those endless stories I have to listen to, but mostly it's because of nervousness."

Well, I said it! Now she knows the truth.

Grace took her hand away from her chin and offered him consolation. "You're not alone in these feelings. Let me propose something that will start both of us in the right direction. I don't want to rush you into anything too soon. I'd like us to meet on a one-to-one basis for awhile. In time, if I think you'd benefit from being in the group, I'd like you to agree to try it. If you have problems staying in the group, we can discuss other options. This way, we'll both commit ourselves to doing the right thing. Would you be agreeable to that?"

A plan so reasonable! She always wins.

It was his choice. She hadn't twisted his arm, so why agree to it, he wondered. The best he could do was to accept her proposal without being committed to staying in the group. "I'll agree to try it. I can't promise any more than that."

She looked pleased. "There are five young people in the group, all cross addicted. They're working hard to stay clean from drugs and alcohol. No one is on medication. I can tell you this: They're all struggling at least as hard as you are."

He didn't want to hear this.

Why the hell is she telling me all this, as if I'm already part of the group?

Grace said more about the young people, but Will couldn't relate to their plight of being even worse off than he was and not on medication. He wasn't about to get emotionally caught up in the lives of those druggies, which is how he saw them.

They're not part of my life and I don't wish to make them part of it. I have my own problems, he thought, but did not say.

When it became clear that Will was not interested in hearing more about the group, Grace paused and said, "Let's not go beyond where we are now. We'll take it one step at a time."

That phrase irritated him even though he understood how it shaped the lives of every recovering alcoholic. One day at a time, one step at a time, one fucking everything at one fucking time. They all had to learn how *not* to dwell on the past, how *not* to worry themselves into a frenzy about the future, how *not* to think the worst thought of all—of never again having a drink. But, the truth was that, like all his AA fellows, he needed to stop thinking ahead and make an effort to concentrate on this day and take the rest of them one at a time.

Grace was already setting the tone for the next meeting. "Next time, I should have Dr. Worthington's report and we can go over that."

Sure, he thought. *Now let me out of here.*

Will left Grace's office feeling dejected and angry, despite the fact that the session had started out so well. He reflected on his feelings on the drive home and realized that he had begun to feel uncomfortable the moment she asked him to join the group. Now, it crossed his mind that the honeymoon with Grace might be over.

CHAPTER 10

Forgiveness

Leaving the firm the previous winter was a turning point in Will Valentine's life. Frank Sasso had promised that his position would still be there when he sobered up. Frank had been good to him, and Will knew that it was better to quit than embarrass himself and Frank, but the humiliation of quitting was more painful than anything he had experienced, even his near death from alcohol poisoning a few months later. For years, he was the runaway train heading for a crash that ultimately brought him to the brink of death. When he saw his bleak future, he knew that he had some pretty tough choices to make if he chose to live.

Will had become a mystery to himself. He was the educated professional with all the fixings for success, and if the social indicators were correct he needed only to perform well. He well knew the seriousness of showing up at the office under the influence of alcohol but he did it anyway. Alcohol took his marriage and his career; both were lost by the time he understood the complexities of alcohol addiction: that recovery meant more than sobering up occasionally.

Now, after months of sobriety, returning to work was still not possible unless anxiety could be brought under control. This was Will's goal. He was depending on Grace Manning to help him accomplish it.

Grace's door was open when he entered the waiting room.

"Will?" She called out.

"Hello, Grace," he said, hanging his jacket on the coat rack.

"Come on in," she said.

He wedged the diary into his seat and Grace took her place on the yellow throne, which seemed less impressive without the sun's reflection.

"Dr. Worthington tells me your meeting went well."

"Yes, at least he put a name on it. Moderate to severe anxiety. Some depression, probably of long-standing."

"Yes, I know. As he told you, he'll be monitoring the medication as we continue to meet. He'll do the follow up as long as you're on medication. You'll still come here regularly. "

"I feel better just knowing I have a real condition. Putting a name on it takes the mystery out of it. Too bad the medication could take six to eight weeks to be effective."

"Yes, that's the down side of these medications. In the meantime, you may want to use the relaxation technique I showed you last time. Try to attend an AA meeting as often as you can. How are you doing with that?"

"I don't go as often as I should," he said, candidly. "I was doing better when I first started out in the program, but now, it's too much for me."

"How so?" she asked.

"When people start talking about their stories, I just don't care to listen."

Grace caught him up on that remark.

"You know Will, for some people it's important to say the words. It's part of the whole process. Sometimes the spoken word brings whatever they're experiencing out in the open where healing can take place. Healing doesn't take place in a vacuum. I know that some people ramble on out of nervousness, but that's just being human. Maybe you can work on becoming more tolerant. I think you have a lot to offer. You're an educated man with a good sense of humor and a nice way about you. People would listen to you. Sometimes when you help someone else you end up helping yourself. "

Will softened. "I hear what you're saying. Maybe I need to heal up a little more before exposing myself to someone else's pain."

Grace looked serious. "I hear you, but try to understand what's really happening in those meetings. Everyone there is trying to build a new life. It's not easy to make the transition. You're part of the process just by being there.

"Some people find it helpful to write about their experiences," she added. "Writing puts what we've experienced in perspective. If you take time to write about the past events of your life a little at a time, you'll be less likely to feel anxious about them when they surface unexpectedly, particularly in the middle of the night."

"I've been reading some pretty interesting stuff in a diary I found in the street, next to my car—about someone in recovery."

He held up the book.

"Oh?" she said.

"It was lying practically under the wheel of my car. There's only a first name. I put an ad in the Lost & Found, hoping to find the owner. It's heady stuff, like nothing I've ever read before. I'd like to know what you think of it."

Grace thumbed through the pages, then started at the beginning and read for a few moments while Will remained silent.

"You're right," she agreed, "pretty heady stuff. It appears to be written by someone who's well into the recovery process. This is some coincidence, Will. What do you make of it?"

"As far as I can see, it's right on the money," he said. "It's poetic and imaginative, an arty kind of thing. I'd sure like to know who she is. She's tough on truth, describing how the mind always reveals the truth, no matter what. She says it'll gnaw at you in so many ways. Still, she says, discerning truth about ourselves isn't the hardest part. The hardest part is accepting it once it's in front of you."

Grace handed him the book. "Well, I see no harm in reading it. It could be of value to you while you're on your own journey. Maybe it will help you be more tolerant of going to meetings," she remarked, smiling.

"That may be expecting too much," he replied with a chuckle, his hand grasping his chin.

"Well, as you go on with the diary, we can discuss some parts of it if you like. If it feels right, keep on with it."

Winding down the session, Grace asked him to start thinking about meeting with the group. He was dreading it, but having agreed to it he would keep his word.

"I'll think about it. I'd like a little more time before I start with the group, if that's okay with you."

Fortunately, she didn't push the matter, and he left her office feeling a reprieve.

He stopped off at the market and bought household cleaning agents with the full intention of giving the apartment a good going over. When he arrived home, he listened to a message from Blair, something about a trip to South America, and he called her right away. She had her own life to live, but at the moment he didn't want her to be so far away.

"Hi, I just got in," she said hearing his voice.

"What's this about South America?"

"I just got the word. I'm going to Peru to do a follow-up on the story the paper initiated. The political situation is unraveling and we want to keep up with what we started a few months ago."

"When do you leave?"

"Tuesday," she replied. "I'll only be away for a couple of weeks. Let's get together on the weekend at Mom's. I'm having dinner with her on Friday, so why not come over and we can all be together. How are you feeling?"

"Not too bad," he replied. "I'm doing some part-time work for Frank, but that's not enough to keep me occupied. I can't wait for this damn medication to kick in."

"Work helps take you out of yourself," she remarked. "But you need to get stronger to do it full time."

When he got off the phone, Will had trepidations about her being so far away. He was too embarrassed to admit the unnerving feeling that had begun to wear on him almost daily. He rallied, nevertheless, and enjoyed seeing Blair and his mother for dinner on Friday. Soon after, Blair left for Peru.

The rest of the week dragged. He met with Grace again and she wasted no time asking him about joining the group in a couple of weeks. "We'll have one more session and then you'll meet with the group. Is that okay?"

He couldn't go back on his promise, so he agreed. She pressed him about attending AA meetings. "Let's review where you are with processing the twelve steps."

"I might have to start from scratch," he said. "I never really processed the first three steps."

"Those steps are not easy," she admitted.

"I keep thinking I can control myself with will power," he admitted. "But when I read the diary, I think she's right about the limitation of will power, and then I perceive the steps differently. She's become my sidekick."

"I'm glad you're finding her diary helpful," Grace replied.

"I can't seem to let go and submit, so to speak. It may be impossible for someone like me to do that. When I first started the program, I was so turned off hearing people in the program talk about submitting to the higher power and being saved. My mind doesn't work that way. What are they trying to be saved from? You'd think they'd want to keep whatever power they have and not give it up."

"Well, they might be seeking help," Grace offered. "Maybe they want to be accepted and forgiven for the weakness of being human. But, go on with what you were saying."

"She writes about faith. Amazing—Faith writing about faith. She says it builds in us. Listen to this," he said, turning to a page in the diary.

I let myself go and slip into the stream. I leave behind my small mind that cannot comprehend something greater. Pebbles turn sharp, but the brook feels nothing as it flows all the way to the cemetery and becomes frozen in winter. My mind seeks a neutral state of wanting truth, even as it freely goes off the mark. When I go off the mark, I feel guilt, but what is it that causes guilt? I think truth denied causes guilt.

The mind does nothing but think. It strives to be greater than it is, but it cannot be greater and I see a serpent biting its tail. In special moments, I am taken to another realm, as when the morning sun steals across my pillow and takes me to a stream far beyond. I am touched by something from another world.

My mind is wary because faith binds me to another realm and stays with me even as hope comes and goes. It takes my heavy load without tiring, a great relief for my troubled mind. It gives me rest. It allows me to work on my troubles one at a time without being overcome by what I have done to myself.

Will lifted his eyes to comment on what he'd just read. "She sees the mind the way I do, except that she gives herself over to faith, and that's where we're different. I like what she says about the way the mind is suspicious. Listen to what she says further down."

> *The mind is not stupid. It is even aware of its limitations, but it envies faith. It becomes nervous when the eternal mystery is bound to faith, not reason. When the mind closes up the conduit of faith, it becomes an icy glacier, haughty and rigid.*

Grace remained silent, waiting for Will to go on talking.

"It makes me think that faith is a kind of settling . . . you know, settling for the best story we can come up with . . . so we can live with some sense that we're included in the mystery, and not alone. Reading this diary, I was thinking of how people struggle to live with a faith that's handed to them, the way children are taught in Sunday school to piggy back someone else's faith, though not encouraged to build a faith of their own. I suppose a taught faith is okay to get the idea of it running, but a personal faith is what you really need for the darkest times. Maybe faith enables us to live with the mystery without having to explain it. The mind is driven toward reason and so it rejects faith. If there is any certainty at all, it's that we all live in the mystery."

"Interesting, both simple and complicated," Grace added. "Faith gives us the freedom to move on, to budge out of the frozen state of that icy glacier. I suppose faith allows us to move forward, even refusing a drink at a critical moment. Faith is telling you that will power alone is not enough for some people. When will power weakens, faith may be what causes you to go to an AA meeting rather than stay home and brood."

"I'm still working on it," Will said, pulling air through his teeth. "So far, I haven't done my best at AA meetings, but life isn't over yet."

Grace laughed, but said nothing, and waited for him to embellish on that comment.

"Maybe someday I'll find a fit at one of those meeting, but I'm not there yet," he admitted. "Right now, I'm struggling with the forgiveness thing. Something keeps getting in the way."

"What gets in the way?" Grace probed.

"Well, I can't put my finger on it exactly. It feels like, you know, what's done is done and there's no going back except with wishful thinking."

Grace interjected. "Those next four steps point you in the direction of taking a moral inventory. We can't hide from the past, so this is a way of being accountable for how we lived our lives. We must reconcile our weakness with the best image we want of ourselves. That's the reality. It does us no good to ignore our weaknesses or to beat ourselves into the ground over them."

"That makes me think of something else I read in the diary . . . about wrestling herself to the ground."

"She may be struggling to forgive herself," Grace remarked.

"Yeah," he said, pensively.

"Forgiveness is freeing," Grace affirmed. "Taking a moral inventory is healthy for anyone, not just people in AA."

"Yeah. Makes me wonder how many people could actually do the steps. It's going to take me a lot longer than I thought."

Suddenly, Will felt drained, and he was glad when Grace summed it all up.

"The next steps," she said, "are devoted to taking action. That eighth step is pivotal. But you're not there yet. For now, why not just think about the first three steps. Don't try to take them in all at once. They're not meant to be memorized, but processed. We'll talk about this again next time. I think we covered enough ground for today."

It wasn't until Will got home that he put his finger on why he was so bothered about forgiveness, asking for forgiveness from others as well as forgiving himself. It was just before Barbara had filed for the divorce. He had been consuming over a quart of vodka each day and eating dinner without even knowing what he was eating and then falling asleep in front of the TV. For a long while, Barbara waited to give him dinner and the usual argument, but in time, he came home to leftovers and ate dinner alone. Too drunk to heat up the only food he would have for the day, he ate it cold and fell asleep on the couch, unaware that Barbara had moved her sleeping place to the sun room. They were no longer spending time together as a family. At some point, when the arguing stopped, they had nothing more to say to each other.

Only now did he realize that something had been building up in the dark recesses of his mind. Demons were stirring. And so it might have been predicted that one day he would find himself crawling up the stairs to the bedroom, a blind mole groping in the dark for a place to bed down. Now he was confronting the demons that had overtaken him. Forgiveness was a long way off.

CHAPTER 11

The Gift

"You can't overturn everything," Dr. Worthington was saying. "Many things come into play after getting sober. Your entire life can't be grasped at once. It's better to start with a small piece, say from a particular event or year and work from there."

Will surmised where Worthington was going and he didn't want to go there. He remained quiet and listened to what he was saying.

"Dr. Manning will be able to help you with matters regarding the twelve steps. Here, we can try to get to the underlying problems of anxiety and depression."

Will was nervous, feeling that Worthington was closing in on him. It was not going to be easy opening up to him. He had never talked to anyone but Blair about some portions of his childhood, but she was family. What was the point of rehashing raw points from so long ago that constituted nothing more than ordinary disappointments in life. It seemed unmanly to whine now about being stuck out in the rural part of town where nothing happened except planting and sowing and fixing machinery.

Surprisingly, Worthington was sympathetic.

"You're not here to blame anything or anyone," he maintained. "It's worthwhile to consider your life and people in it so that you may understand yourself better. It's like constructing the unique puzzle that makes up the picture of Will Valentine. In therapy, we hope to relieve the burdens that hinder us, but first they need to surface. Keep in mind that there's a great difference between laying blame and laying groundwork."

Will didn't care how well Worthington put it. He just didn't like talking about his parents, especially to someone who had never met them. Their honor was at stake. In retrospect, when Will had time to mull over this conversation, he thought it was clever the way Worthington got him to talk about his family by asking if he had come home from the Army with thoughts of becoming an architect.

"I think my father had envisioned me in the family business. Not that he pushed it. I just knew in my heart that that's what he wanted. Looking back, I think I must have struggled with that. I really wanted to be on my own, away from the neighborhood, but I couldn't admit that then. Machine repair was okay, but I never wanted to make it my life's work. My father thought I had a talent for it, or maybe he simply wanted me to like it. I know he felt satisfied after repairing someone's machine or taking a sheet of metal and fashioning it into something worthwhile.

"There's a rewarding feeling that comes after seeing something through from start to finish. But I experience that with my drawings."

"So, when you came home from the Army, then what?" Worthington asked.

"I got a job with a small architectural firm. I could draw anything, just an inborn talent. Once I was there I knew that's where I wanted to be. I saved enough money to study further. By then, I was a grown man, and I wanted to be on my own. The Army had changed me."

"Then what?" Worthington asked.

"Well, I got hired by Sasso & Fern, the firm that I left last year. Then, I met a pretty blond and we got married, and then my daughter was born. I was drinking regularly, but it didn't become a problem until I was stopping at the bar at the end of the day instead of coming directly home. At first, it was once or twice a week. I used the excuse that I was giving Barbara time to finish up the day with Samantha. Barbara wasn't happy with that. At some point, the drinking became heavy. It took a long time for all the air to go out of our marriage, ten years to be exact. I couldn't seem to turn things around."

"How did your parents take to that?" Worthington asked.

"When I was drinking heavily, I kept away from them. I'm sure they knew things weren't going well but they never said anything. They weren't the type to probe into our lives. But I know they were hurting, and so was my sister. Blair never caused them any worry. She got a full scholarship to college and always did everything right. There was only one asshole in the family and it was me."

"It's just the two of you, you and your sister?" Worthington asked.

"Yes," Will replied. She's two years older.

"So, what prompted the break-up after those ten stormy years?"

"I had made a habit of always working late and stopping off at the bar instead of coming home. One night, I punched a guy who started trouble in the bar."

Worthington ran his hand over his chin then adjusted his tie. "How did that come about?"

"The typical bar story—a guy started in on me because he had heard about me and wanted to challenge my boxing skill. There wasn't much boxing involved, more of a swift left hook that ended the fight. When I was sure he was coming at me, I just let him have it with one punch. You get to know the troublemakers. In all the years of going to bars, I never once started a fight or goaded someone into a fight. That may seem hard to believe. Anyway, the guy never knew what hit him. That's when I knew something had to be done about my drinking. My fist was becoming a lethal weapon. I made a weak attempt at rehab."

Will could have gone on talking but time was running out, and besides, he had said enough for the session.

Worthington checked his watch. "I'd like to hear more about that. Let's pick up on this again next time."

CHAPTER 12

Holding On

Will was concerned about Faith, afraid that if she couldn't make it then there might be little hope for him. The words in her diary indicated that she was in trouble.

The brook is frozen. Blue ice has stiffened my lips. I cannot speak. Cars come through this graveyard without stopping. The caretaker moves silently in his cold shadow waiting for the faucets to flow. Who knows what he carries from one grave to another. No one is there to check his credentials. Cars drive away. No flowers are left behind. I'm caught by the plummeting cold.

Don't despair, he wanted to say to her. He turned the page and read further.

My will grows weak. I dream of the neon light, a beacon in the night time sky, playing on my weakness and desire, daring my life. I open the door and death greets me in sheep's clothing. I must find my way home before the circuitry closes down. Alcohol has always kept me from the dark halls of my mind. Now, there are choices to be made. I wrestle myself to the ground. I feel my mind burning at the edges of its freedom. In sleep, I wander through fields of incongruities where dreams take shape from infinite bundling and swapping of synapses. Is it better to be asleep or to be awake?

Anxiety and depression were getting the best of Will even though he was taking medication. The diary no longer soothed him. He worried about Faith and feared she might be dead and, therefore, couldn't claim the diary. She wrote about having choices to make at every turn, but she also said that hope comes out of nowhere. Maybe she has made it out alive, he thought, and he searched the diary for a glimmer of hope.

Water keeps me moving out of myself. My mind floats. In a fleeting moment, there is being without dimension, a magnitude unbound, a being, all knowing, as infinitely small as infinitely great. There is nothing like this in my imagination. I exist in an out-of-body experience. The more I try to hold onto the experience and grasp the moment, the quicker it slips away. I cannot form it into an image.

My mind knows that it lacks perfection, but this lack seems not to diminish the truth it is capable of discerning, which truth is perfect. What makes me strive for truth? I wish to be released from imperfection, to be taken away by each new sunrise, out of the endless circle of my mind, which is destined to repeat theme upon theme, motif upon motif, life upon life, death upon death, in a never-ending process of myth.

Will was tempted to cancel his appointment with Dr. Worthington out of frustration with the medication. He felt no relief from anxiety and now he feared the medication wasn't working for him. He wasn't in a frame of mind to unravel his past with Worthington as he had on the previous visit, yet what would he gain by canceling the appointment?

He decided to bring the diary with him to read in the waiting room. When he came to the part he was looking for, he read it again trying to find hope for himself.

My mind is fragile despite its strength, losing courage at its limits. The temporal mind is limited, yet is obsessed with the notion of the eternal. I imagine the future but I am driven to think backward from the present, ending up in a never-ending circle. My mind wants what it can't have, causing me to think and desire according to my limitations.

A sparrow peeps as it hops on the walk, and for a brief moment hope pours into the recesses of my mind and my troubled circuitry becomes free. Sometimes, the feeling only lasts for a few seconds, long enough to remind me that relief is in the offing. I wonder where hope comes from, if not from my own mind. Hope comes and goes and nourishes faith the way a breath of fresh air revitalizes my lungs.

"Coffee?" the receptionist asked.

"Yes, thanks. Black is fine." Will tucked the diary into his pocket.

Dr. Worthington was ready to see him and so Will brought his coffee inside.

"Hi there, Will," Worthington said, coming around to shake hands. "Have a seat. How are you?"

"I'm a bit flat," Will replied, thinking that he should have revealed how awful he was feeling, and that his frustration level was mounting. "So far, I feel no relief from the medication. I think that's what's buggin' me."

"You've been taking it for awhile."

"Yes, and nothing has changed."

"It may be too soon to tell," Worthington said. "I realize it's not easy to be patient when you're feeling like this."

"Especially when I have my full time position waiting for me," Will remarked.

"How's that going?" Worthington inquired.

"I'll be returning to my full time position at Sasso & Fern when I can get the anxiety under control."

"I remember—that's where you began your professional career?"

"Yes. Frank Sasso is not only a colleague but a friend. He gave me a break more than once when I needed it. Last year, I worked on the plans for a major Alzheimer's wing for Sweets Convalescent Home. Everyone called it *the sweet spot*."

Worthington smiled. "And you left the firm last year, right?"

"Yes. I quit rather than stay and get fired. I remember that winter like it was yesterday. For weeks, the temperature was so cold. When I went on site, I parked my car next to a stand of oak trees lining the parking lot of the convalescent home. The dried oak leaves were trying to hang on. They reminded me of the people I saw in the home, trying to hold on, some of them just clinging to life. From my car, I'd watch the leaves flapping in the wind. They were so crisp and brittle, like sculptures of tarnished gold. I had a private bet that the wind wouldn't tug them off."

"Did you win the bet?" Worthington asked.

"Yeah, well they stayed on until February. I don't know what happened to them after that."

Worthington pushed the subject further. "It's a wonder what keeps any life holding on against the odds. Did you see the Alzheimer's patients?"

Will described what he had seen there. "Yes, when I went on site to check my plans I met many of them. That was an experience! I don't know what kept them hanging on. One afternoon, while I was reviewing my drawings, I saw a man I had known over the years in construction. He started taking off his clothing and removing his teeth, like I wasn't there. What struck me was that his eyes didn't appear vacant but looked determined and fully engaged in what he was doing. It's like someone else comes along and fills your shoes and the stranger left behind is in fact the empty shell of yourself."

"You witnessed what most people never see unless a family member has the disease," Worthington added.

They sat for a moment, not saying anything, and then Worthington broke the silence.

"So, when will that new wing be built?"

"They'll be breaking ground in late spring. I'm sure I'll hear about it from Frank Sasso. But, I can't return to work until I get the anxiety under control. I wouldn't want a repeat of what I went through last year."

"What was it like?" Worthington asked, sounding like a regular guy, and that loosened Will up to say more.

"At first I could handle things. Frank Sasso allowed me to keep my own schedule without putting pressure on me. But, I was drinking during the day. Even then, drinking was no longer an enjoyment but a means to quiet anxiety. I knew I was in trouble when the mellowing effect decreased and the alcohol consumption increased. You know how it is. The handwriting was on the wall."

"I understand," he said. "So you were drinking before coming to work—every day?"

Will gave a full account to Worthington of how he had stopped at the bar every morning before going to the office and poured eight shots of vodka into a tumbler of cranberry juice and drank it down.

"You know, in long swigs. My body took it in like medicine. In a few minutes my nervous system would quiet down enough for me to face going to work. I did this for weeks, until I couldn't keep up with the demands of the job and had to face the truth: that I was a chronic alcoholic, all day, all night, everyday, all the time."

Worthington's brow drew taut. "Surely, it was impossible to keep that kind of drinking from being noticed."

"Yeah. I kept thinking, if I could just hold off in the morning long enough to get my work done, I could go to Sonny's . . . that's the bar I went to. I felt humiliated by my weakness of not being able to handle the daily pressures of work like other people. But, I couldn't handle being on edge, sometimes even panicky."

"Is that the kind of nervousness you're feeling now?" Worthington asked.

"Just about. The only difference is that I'm healthy and I'm not drinking. But, I'm afraid the next drink is just around the corner and that could be my last if you know what I mean. Last year, when the anxiety was at its worst, I'd drink a couple of beers in the morning to quiet my stomach before going to the bar, and when I got to the bar I'd drink pep-permint schnapps to get my stomach ready so I could throw down a tumbler of vodka and cranberry juice. I needed that amount of alcohol just to get rolling. What a case!"

"It's a real dilemma when alcohol is both the disease and the remedy," Worthington remarked.

"Yeah, what I wanted was killing me. I'd measure out an exact amount of alcohol each day, just enough to quiet me. I could have died from the amount I was throwing down and yet in a real sense I was as careful as a pharmacist measuring out drugs. I knew that I needed a certain amount for it to be effective and that more would kill me. I remember trying to drink only what I needed in a twenty-four hour period. That's when I realized I was using alcohol as a medication. But you didn't have to be a rocket scientist to detect Vodka on my breath or see it in my eyes."

"That was some balancing act," Worthington recognized, "drinking enough to quiet anxiety without altogether poisoning yourself."

"Yeah, I did that until February," Will admitted. "I knew my days at the firm were numbered. Frank Sasso had already taken me aside. He knew I was using alcohol to control anxiety. But, he had a responsibility to his staff and to the clients. He asked me to try to get it under control."

"It appears that he tried to do his best for you."

"Frank is a class act. No one could have changed the situation but me. I just wasn't ready to do it. I continued believing that I could make it if I could work in the morning and go to the bar in the late afternoon and stay until dinner time, you know, so I could drink just the amount I needed before going home."

"Sounds like you were beginning to have a dialogue with yourself," Worthington stated, his perceptiveness pleasing Will.

"Looking back, I guess that's true. While I still wasn't able to admit to being an all out alcoholic, I knew that I needed a certain amount of alcohol to quiet the nervousness. It's just that it took a long while for me to connect the dots. What an ass-hole!"

"How long did you go on like that after leaving the job?"

"About three months, until May. I left my office one night in February and on the way to Sonny's I suddenly made the decision to quit work. It came as a relief, like the struggle was finally over, probably like the way death brings relief from lifelong struggle. When it became impossible to get through the morning without alcohol I thought—why put myself through this? I just knew it was time to leave. While I was driving to Sonny's the night I left work all I could think of was my father and how disciplined he was."

"How much did he know about your addiction?" Worthington asked.

"He probably saw my drinking as a weakness but I don't think he understood addiction as we know it. My father lived a regulated life. At the end of the day, he would sit with my mother and they'd have a beer before supper and talk about their day. Occasionally he had a beer in the evening. But he never went to a bar. I mean he would have been like a fish out of water in a bar. He drank the way he lived his life . . . regulated. He told me he didn't mind if I drank as long as I drank in moderation. If he could have seen me last year . . ."

"You mentioned that your father had passed away." Will was impressed that Worthington had remembered everything that was said.

"Yes. And as much as I miss him, at least he wasn't around for the fallout."

"When you drove over to the bar after leaving work, you said that you felt your tension relax. Can you recall more about that?" Worthington inquired.

"I remember the cold February air and my mind clear as a bell. Everything was rushing at me as I was driving and I realized I was no longer having the fun I'd had when alcohol gave me pleasure. It bothered me that my life was reduced to two states: anxiety with no alcohol and oblivion with alcohol. I wasn't kidding myself. I mean, I needed a quart of vodka to reach the desired numb state. I was scared, wishing only that I could reach that state with less booze.

"On the drive to Sonny's I opened the car window and let the cold air hit my face. I hadn't felt hungry in a long time and when I saw Burger King I pulled into the drive-thru and ordered a Whopper. I sat in the parking lot and devoured it like I just couldn't get it in fast enough. It was the most enjoyable food I'd had in weeks. I drove out into the street like a stranger escaping into the night, and the closer I got to Sonny's Place, the more I felt my life pouring back into me."

"There's something about the bar that keeps people coming back. The red neon lights, the environment, like a cocoon," Worthington remarked.

"Yeah," Will agreed, his eyes lighting up. "And, you're not alone. Everyone is in the same boat. In a good bar, you can talk if you want to or you can just sit and listen to what's going on and shoot the breeze with the bartender."

"Those months from February to May, when you were out of work, what were they like?"

"Well, to complicate matters, at the end of February I left Sonny's and took a different route home to drop off a friend who needed a ride. As I was turning into his street, I collided with an oncoming car and lost my license - DWI. So, then I was not only without a job but without a car. It seemed my whole life was converging on me.

"Then, in March, well, I was still drinking continuously and my sister later told me that I was speaking in what sounded like slow motion, like I was about to check out. I don't know how I was able to walk to Sonny's every day. I remember forcing myself to appear strong so some asshole wouldn't try to take advantage of me. My sister phoned me every evening because she was afraid I was going to die. We had recently re-established our relationship. We were always close but we hadn't seen each other much when I was really . . . you know, three sheets to the wind. She always kept in touch with my daughter in Michigan. Blair's not a drinker and she tried to understand my addiction logically. She's a problem solver type and she kept on suggesting all sorts of remedies I might try, but I couldn't hear any of it.

"Everyone at Sonny's knew how bad I was. My friend, Ritchie, tried to get me to go to the hospital. He sat with me at the bar and I remember telling him, 'You can sit here with me if you want to, but don't try to get me to go through de-tox. I'm not ready. I can't do it.' My face felt paralyzed and I could hardly make my voice heard. Ritchie and I sat there drinking until Sonny was ready to close. I was in bad shape. Ritchie knew how serious it was. He offered to drive me home, and I made him promise not to talk anymore about going to the V.A. hospital, which is where he ultimately took me. I could hardly make it up the stairs to the garden apartment I was living in at the time. Ritchie came inside and said he'd just stay awhile. He told me later that he knew I wouldn't have made it through the night, that he'd never seen me that low. Anyway, we sat together for a while, and then, suddenly, the words came out. I just said, 'I guess I'm ready.'"

Will's eyes glistened as he recalled that fateful night. Worthington said nothing and waited for Will to compose himself.

"Anyway, Ritchie drove me to the hospital and brought me directly to the de-tox unit. I was supposed to stay five days and then be transferred to another wing for the full program. But, during the five days, my body responded quickly to nourishment and medication. I steadily regained strength.

"Once I was out of danger, I decided not to be admitted for the long haul. There's something about confinement that makes me feel like a caged animal. I talked my daughter out of taking time off from work and flying from Michigan to see me. Blair helped out. She stocked me up with food and looked in on me. Alcoholics can always get the people they love to do things for them. She asked me to promise never to drink alcohol again. All I could tell her was that I would only make promises I could keep.

"Here I was, only a few days from being at death's door, and still I couldn't bring myself to say that I'd never drink again. I couldn't admit that I had no control over the urge to drink. Even then, I remember telling Blair that I thought I could drink in moderation, that I'd never tried drinking in moderation before. I thought I could pace myself and have a little white wine, nothing more than that. She didn't try to argue with me but I'm sure she knew that a few sips of wine would do me in as easily as a case of Vodka. Looking back, I was just conning myself, bargaining with the devil. Blair later told me that she thought I had to take myself to the mat one more time, and that she promised herself not to interfere with it.

"Well, it took less than three days of drinking *a little white wine* to put me back in the condition I was in two weeks before. Alcohol had become a poison for me.

"My daughter . . . that's Samantha, phoned from Michigan one night and told me she loved me whether I drank or not.

She said, "You're not the only person in the world who uses alcohol to relieve anxiety, but you're my only father.

Your life is worth everything to me. I wish your life meant as much to you as it does to me."

"Something clicked after that. I was able to understand that I got caught in the trap of using alcohol to relieve nervousness and then becoming a full blown alcoholic. I was starting to understand that anxiety had plagued me all my life and talking about it freed me up. Samantha said, 'in the end, what does it matter if anxiety caused you to drink alcohol or that alcohol caused you to be addicted? You're a full-blown alcoholic with anxiety and both conditions have to be treated.'

"The rest is history. In May, I began treatment at the outpatient clinic. That's when I moved to the south end. I didn't have my license because of DWI so on days when I couldn't get a ride I could bus over to the clinic.

"I'd be interested in hearing how you adjusted to the program," Worthington said. "Maybe next time we can talk about that."

Will looked at his watch and found that fifty-minutes had already gone by. It felt more like fifteen minutes and he had done all the talking.

Blair phoned once while she was in Peru. She sounded upbeat. Her assignment was going well and there was no point in sounding needy when she was so far away. It was not just the anxiety getting him down but also the frustration of making so little progress with the twelve steps. Chichi kept on asking him to come over to the Italian club, always showing sensitivity to *the drink*, as he referred to Will's addiction.

"Have a ginger ale, Will, play a little cards. Bocci Luigi keeps askin' 'where's Will?'"

But even that was too much. Wherever he went he felt like a fish out of water. Everything he enjoyed he couldn't have. Full time work was too much for him. Going to Sonny's would be a disaster. With no place to land safely he was miserable. All he could do was wait for the medication to kick in.

The following week, Grace introduced him to the people in the group. They were young and addicted to hard drugs and alcohol. He felt sorry for a young woman who said she had no *clean* home to go to. Grace was right . . . the baggage they carried was even heavier than his.

Initially, he shared nothing about his personal life, believing that what mattered to him would be of no interest to them. Yet, as he showed concern for their dual addiction problems, the more they wanted to hear what he had to say. The chemistry worked to Grace's liking and she remarked to him at the end of one session, "The group is better off with you in it."

He phoned Dr. Worthington a second time to complain about the medication, and once again the dosage was increased. He didn't hold back from telling Worthington what he thought about the way he was being treated.

"The way I see it," he told Worthington on the phone, "everyone's cold-turkey oriented. What's the difference if I take a possibly addictive medication if my only other option is alcohol? I can't go on like this."

Worthington wouldn't budge. "Grace Manning thinks you could be working on the twelve steps more diligently."

"No one seems to understand that I can't participate more in the program until the anxiety is under control. I want to get back to work and start living a normal life. I can't work feeling like this and I can't sit through anymore damn AA meetings."

When the phone call ended, Will felt dejected and it even crossed his mind that Grace might have betrayed him by revealing that he was not working the steps as well as he could. He had been honest with her about going to Sonny's each morning to read the newspaper and drink coffee, and she didn't hold her tongue when she told him that it demonstrated poor judgment. Their bond was based on respect, honesty and trust. He was feeling sorry for himself in his misery and worse for even thinking that Grace had betrayed him.

A time bomb was ticking and in a matter of time it would likely go off.

CHAPTER 13

Money in the Bank

Will was telling Worthington about his first weeks in recovery, speaking freely now after their many sessions together. Medication was still a sore point between them but now they were talking man to man.

"I had enough money in the bank to pay for a high-priced recovery center, but I didn't want to leave town, and from what I heard later, those places don't do much more than what can be accomplished by attending AA meetings in local communities. I didn't need such comfort and I really didn't care if anyone knew I was in recovery. So, anyway, my program began on a positive note. I was committed to living one day at a time. Classes were held five days a week and I had no license because of the DWI. During the first week, I wasn't feeling strong, but then I got to enjoy taking an occasional long walk home to think things through. After being cooped up all day, the fresh air felt good.

"Sometimes, Blair picked me up and I'd have dinner at her house. With Blair, I could talk freely about the program.

There were lots of adjustments. There was Walter, an old-timer, who was always on me. He'd single me out and ask, 'How many AA meetings do you attend?' I told him that I try to make as many meetings as possible, maybe three or four a week, and he said, 'Well, from now on, I want you to attend five meetings a week.'

"I wanted so much to put him in short pants, but I held back. I explained that it was hard for me to attend more meetings because I had these other meetings to go to, like DWI. He knew I was up to my ears in meetings. But, the *son-of-a-bitch* wouldn't back off and he seemed to enjoy wielding his power in front of the others.

"Then he asked, 'How many days a week did you drink?' I was honest in telling him that I drank seven days a week. He actually pointed his finger at me and said, 'Well then, I want you to attend *seven* AA meetings a week.' Can you believe they have a loser like that working with people who are there seeking help?"

Worthington nodded and released a wry smile, indicating that he understood Will's frustration. "Did Walter pick on anyone else or just you?"

"He'd go after others, too. In group sessions, he'd provoke someone and get an argument going and then he'd watch it play out. He was acting on an inflated ego, trying to be the professional he was not. I had all I could do to hold back. He didn't know how close he came to being in the hospital.

"Good thing I had Blair to talk to."

"What did she think of him?" Worthington asked.

"She kept reminding me that there are hundreds of Walters out there and that I had to learn to deal with them without my fist. 'Just put up with it for a few more weeks,' she'd say. 'At least, you don't have to see him every day.'"

Worthington smiled. "She was right, of course. Some people will get under your skin if you let them."

"It's just that I was a captive audience for Walter. I mean I couldn't get out of his face. What I wanted most was to challenge him to a duel. The only thing stopping me was the thought of being thrown out of the program. It's a wonder Walter didn't drive me to drink."

Worthington laughed. "How did you relate to the others in the group?"

"My patience was tested in those group sessions, listening to those stories and then having to rev up again to attend AA evening meetings. The young people in my group were cross-addicted . . . you know, alcohol, cocaine, heroin. I couldn't see how they could make it. Most of them had no clean home to go to. I knew when they were using, and so did the counselor leading our group. I mean, sooner or later, they'd be found out from their weekly urine samples. At first, I couldn't relate to their problems. I had enough of my own. It's not that I was looking for sympathy but I couldn't find anyone who would recognize *my* dual problem . . . of alcohol and anxiety. I still see it as a dual problem."

Worthington nodded and lifted his eyebrows in agreement.

"But I've changed since then," Will told him. "It seems now I can't stop talking about myself. Seven months ago, I was like a clam."

"It takes time to come out to others and to feel comfortable doing so. What do you think it was that kept you sober during those early weeks?" Worthington asked.

"Will power," Will blurted out. "That's not what the program recommends, but I think will power alone kept me from drinking. I never sought help from others. I'm used to counting on myself. I'm trying to be more open to the idea of accepting help, but I don't expect to change my basic nature."

"Did you benefit from the anger management sessions?" Worthington asked.

"I went to two sessions and that was enough to get me to see how I had always handled things . . . no pun intended."

Worthington smiled, almost laughed, as Will continued.

"It's not in me to step back from a fight when I'm provoked. It was an enlightening experience to hear from other people who had a problem controlling their anger. I'll probably have to work on anger every day until I'm too old to remember what I'm so angry about. In a way, I hate giving it up. It's so much easier to settle things with a left hook, you know, it's quicker and much more satisfying."

Worthington laughed out loud for the first time. "It's just that consequences sometimes get in the way."

"That's true. If it weren't for consequences, I wouldn't be here." Will replied.

Will found it was easier to get along with Worthington when they could laugh. He still perceived him as a funny sort of duck, but he was getting to like him. Worthington wanted to know how he had handled sobriety when the program ended and the ten-week DWI class was over.

"I made the mistake of thinking that my work was done, but I found out otherwise. I went to Arizona to visit a girlfriend . . . just a friend. I was looking forward to the visit, but something began gnawing at me as soon as I arrived in Sedona. I stayed with the woman for a week but only out of kindness. All the while I could feel anxiety building up. I couldn't shake it. It affected everything I did. It was then that I knew I would drink again. I didn't know *when* I would drink, only that I would drink if the anxiety became intolerable. It was like having money in the bank. I couldn't face living like that the rest of my life, living in an emotional hell without drinking. I made a pact with myself: I'd wait until I couldn't take it anymore, and then I'd drink. I felt better just knowing that."

"Was that when you began thinking about medications?" Worthington asked.

"I think it was right around that time. Yes. That's when I knew I needed something more than will power and more than AA meetings. But, as you know, program people aren't in favor of medications. I knew that a psychiatrist would have to diagnose my condition and prescribe a medication, but all that seemed so far out of my reach. Alcohol was readily available, so close at hand, and I knew it so well."

Will shook his head. "Besides, I wasn't in favor of seeing a *shrink*, if you'll excuse the expression . . ."

Worthington smiled and said, "I've been called that before."

The clock was running out and they needed to end the session.

"As you said, Will, you've come a long way. Only months ago you were facing this alone and now you have abundant support. Let's see how it goes from here."

"I've never believed much in miracles, but who knows?" Will quipped.

"Well, look at you now, talking to a psychiatrist," Worthington observed. "That's one proof that the impossible can become possible."

CHAPTER 14

296 Days to Day 1

A little wine was all he needed to calm the anxiety. The self-fulfilling prophecy had been his stalking horse since the trip to Sedona, and now it was time to give in to it. Will power, be damned! It was time to take matters into his hands. Will set out for Sonny's Place and drank a beer, then another. The next day he tried some wine and soon he was ready for his old standby—vodka and cranberry juice. He drank for a few more days without attaining the calm he was looking for.

On the fifth day, he could hardly climb the stairs to his apartment. No one knew what was happening except Cozy who licked his face as he took the stairs one at a time. Will didn't return phone calls from his sister or his mother and he remained alone in his misery except for visits from his faithful friend, Cozy. Chichi brought food and left it at his door. Blair had sensed there was something else going on with her brother, and she later told him that she only prayed that the outcome this time would be different.

No one but another alcoholic would have understood that he was experiencing the ultimate sorrow: that alcohol didn't work for him anymore. Alcohol had given up on him. Drinking was no longer an option. But, this relapse was different. The long difficult months of going to AA meetings and sessions with Grace Manning and Dr. Worthington had provided him with tools he had never had before. For the first time, he was able to pull himself out of the dark hole and start again; and after two hundred and ninety six days of sobriety, he started counting all over again from day one.

It was the first week of March. In two months, he would have celebrated his first anniversary of sobriety. Having missed his appointment with Grace, he was certain she knew what had happened. He returned to Sonny's Place the next day and phoned her, prepared to admit the truth.

Immediately, she questioned him about the noise in the background.

"It sounds like a bar."

"It *is* a bar," he replied. There was a moment of silence.

"Grace . . . . Are you there?"

"You missed *group*," she replied with a sharp and unfriendly voice.

Shit, she's pulling the socks up on her little boy.

"What happened?" she asked.

"I was drinking," he admitted.

"You know the rule. You can't stay in the group when you're drinking."

"I know, but I'm not drinking now. Last night I made the decision to come back to Sonny's for coffee, not alcohol. I know what the stakes are. I'm asking you to take me back."

Her silence gave him time to say more.

"I want to come back. I want to stay in the group."

Grace wasn't about to put him through a vise, not after he had reached this point on his own. "I'll see you here tomorrow morning at ten," she said firmly, and then hung up.

Grace greeted him the next day with her usual pleasant manner, and she seemed glad to have him back.

"You should be checked out by a doctor. A five-day binge might have killed you. Here's the name of a physician who may be able to fit you in soon. Try to schedule an appointment as soon as possible. And, Will, I want you to really try hard to attend the AA meetings. If you need to talk anything through before we meet next week, call me."

After that binge, it was clear to Will that alcohol would never work for him again, but if not vodka, beer or a little white wine, then *what*? There were moments, days, of anguish. Will was overwhelmed with the thought of having to live the rest of his life sober, like being in someone else's skin. The bottle was deadly but the idea of living without it was unbearable. *Who am I without alcohol*, he thought. His desire to return to full time work had diminished and, once again, his life was on hold.

Grace continued to push him to understand that he was imprisoning himself by relying exclusively on will power. "All the king's horses and all the king's men are not enough," she told him. "You must build something inside yourself besides will power."

In March Will was still meeting regularly with Grace. In all the weeks of taking the medication, his anxiety level never changed.

"What's in store for me if will power and therapy and the most popular drug on the market won't work," he complained to Grace.

He kept his weekly appointments with the group, and when the others didn't show up he saw her privately. Sometimes he felt better after seeing Dr. Worthington, but there were times when they'd spend the better part of fifty minutes looking at each other without accomplishing anything. He had thought Worthington to be a bit strange right from the start. It wasn't something he could put his finger on. Maybe it was just the way he patted down his missing hair or reached for his goddamn tie before addressing the imperatives.

The Indian doctor recommended by Grace was a friendly sort. She gave Will a complete physical and told him his body was in good shape considering the damage it had been subjected to for so many years. She let him know in no uncertain terms that he could have died during the five-day binge.

No shit, he wanted to say.

"Not many people have such a strong constitution," Grace later remarked. "Did she discuss nutrition?"

"She recommended daily multi-vitamins, so I'll be starting each morning with vitamins, orange juice, and a banana. That's not like me."

"Good!" Grace exclaimed. "Poor nutrition is a serious matter for people who drink heavily. You don't want your liver to weaken. When the liver goes, even sobriety doesn't matter anymore. How lucky you are that your body is so forgiving. Why don't you return the favor?"

"I'll try," he said. "I guess everything is relative. If I had a bad liver, I'd be saying that if only I had a good liver I could make it. Here I am with a good liver, and I'm still struggling to make it. Humans are strange creatures."

CHAPTER 15

Nightmares

Will had lost patience with the trial and error method of treatment, and he didn't hold back from telling Dr. Worthington that the medication was not for him, that he was done with it."

To Will's surprise, Worthington agreed. "Some people need to try more than one prescription drug before they find one that is effective. But I agree that this is not the right one for you. I'll start you on another medication, but, of course, only time will tell how effective it is. I can also give you an additional short term medication to help you through the coming weeks."

Guinea pig is what came to Will's mind. As much as he wanted to go off his medication he feared that experimenting for weeks with something new would take too much time and make him vulnerable to alcohol. The full time position was waiting for him at Sasso & Fern. He would have to focus on that; besides, there was little choice in the matter. He started taking the two new medications and braced himself for another round of trial and error, but he couldn't shrug off the feeling that he had taken a downward turn. Cozy came upstairs every day and took his place on the sofa, which helped keep up Will's spirits during Worthington's treatment plan. As much as he was tempted to phone Frank Sasso and tell him that he was ready to return to work full time, he just couldn't face the embarrassment of starting again and failing. And so he didn't call Frank.

He met again with Grace's *druggie* group. Everyone had an opportunity to talk about what had troubled them during the week. About midway through the meeting, great relief came over him, the way he had experienced it in Arizona when he knew he was going to drink. The thought of drinking made him increasingly more cheerful as the meeting continued. He would walk to Sonny's after the meeting and have a beer, nothing more. It was as simple as that!

A rather timid young woman in the group offered to give him a ride home. She was struggling in a desperate situation and he accepted her offer because he felt sorry for her. He would go over to Sonny's after she dropped him off.

She looked tired. Dark circles under her eyes made her look older than her years. He listened to her ramble on about her troubled home life, perturbed that she might have perceived him as a father figure because of a little silver in his hair. But when he saw the look of desperation in her eyes he couldn't ignore her neediness to talk about her situation, which was so much worse than his. She was struggling to keep sober and clean in a home where it was unsafe because, as she put it, her asshole husband smoked pot at night and on weekends, and the son-of-a bitch knew she was having a tough time making it through each day.

Will listened to her go on and on about how recovery would be easier if only she could feel safe in her own home. He thought about all the 'ifs' he had heard people say and realized he had said them too. *If only this, if not that.*

She parked in front of the house, keeping the motor running, and their conversation wound down. Will told her to hang in and try to stay clean no matter what. "Temptations are all around us," he told her. "They'll always be there. It's up to us to know how to keep the shit from landing on us."

She laughed. "But what can we do if it does land on us?"

Will did his best to lift her spirits. "Grow tomatoes."

No sooner than those words left his mouth he felt his age. She gave him a weak smile. "Thanks for listening," she said. "See you next week. If you need a ride, call me."

He wasn't likely to call her for a ride, but he thanked her for the kind offer. He watched the car head down the street and he felt sorry her, so young and with little chance for a happy life unless she could take the heat or leave her husband. Will gave up on the thought of going to Sonny's. Instead, he went upstairs and that's where he remained the rest of the night.

He told Blair about the young woman the next day.

"Funny how one thing comes along and changes the course of everything," she remarked. "Good thing you took the ride."

Will had had a close call and he was scared. For a while, he attended more AA meetings and even forced himself to stay to the end, but there was something about such close proximity with people that made him uncomfortable, and so he made sure to sit in the back of the room in case he needed to make a quick departure. He hoped no one perceived him as antisocial because he genuinely liked people; as he explained to Grace, he just didn't want them taking up his elbow room. When anxiety struck, he had no choice but to keep to himself. He thought it was easier for a man to be perceived as a loner than a nervous Nelly. By now, he was tired of hearing his own words, *if only I could get some relief, I could get on with my life; if only this, if only that.*

The truth was that he was doing no better on the new medication. Bad dreams interrupted his sleep and hope was giving way to despair. He visited his mother and sometimes stayed until ten o'clock just to keep from going home. During the day, he worked on his car and helped Chichi dig the soil to get the garden ready for planting.

"I feel lousy," he told Blair. "I'm shaky and nervous all the time. I hear locusts in my head. It's scary."

She tried to piece together a logical explanation for his feelings. "Just think of all that your brain has been through. The vessels have been exposed to so much alcohol. I think your brain needs to go through a longer healing process."

"I'm sure my brain needs more healing," he agreed, "but I think the noise in my head is from the medication. I didn't have this before. Violent dreams are waking me up every night. No kidding, they terrify me. It takes so long to get back to sleep. I'm sure the sound of locusts in my head is from one of the medications and I even fear having a stroke or a heart attack."

"Dr. Worthington said you could phone anytime," Blair reminded him. "Why not take him up on it?"

Out of desperation, Will saw Worthington a few days later and described the noises in his head that sounded like locusts. Worthington asked about his dreams.

"They're terrifying," Will told him. "Last night, I woke up in a sweat from wild places in Alabama and Tennessee. There were women and money problems and too much partying. People were gambling and I was threatened by motorcycle gangs on the road. Motorcycles were in my head, and teenagers were at my mother's house and it was dark and my father was sleeping. Then suddenly it was Christmas and my father was emptying beer cases, and there was a problem with my drawings. I ran as fast as I could but I got shot anyway and my drawings got wet. I was getting married. There was a violent bloodbath. It started with a basketball game and ended with knives and everyone getting maimed. I found myself in jail with no telephone number and no bond money. There were women, lots of women, and I was hitting a baseball at my mother's house while my father was widening the garage. Mice were running around and locusts were in my head, and I splashed water on my face from the bathroom sink, and I could read the clock backwards. It was 4:44 in the morning."

Worthington took him off the short-term medication but kept him on the other. That night, the wild dreams persisted, and Will felt jumpy all the next day. He took medication late in the afternoon before going to an AA meeting. When the meeting broke, he felt restless and decided on the spur of the moment to go over to Sonny's. He stayed there for half an hour listening to a customer talk to Sonny about a guy's pitching arm. Sonny smiled and nodded. Will listened but didn't say much. Occasionally, Sonny would catch his eye. The guy was full of beer talk, wanting Sonny to think he knew all about pitchers who had the best curve and drop. Sonny knew a lot about baseball and he could have put the guy down with the knowledge he carried in his head; instead he let the guy ramble on. Will, too, could have nailed him with the baseball statistics he hadn't forgotten but he knew enough to follow Sonny's lead and leave the guy alone.

The customer was happy enough when he left. Will couldn't wait to ask Sonny how he could listen to so much bullshit and remain quiet. Sonny smiled. "That's the business I'm in. What good would it do me or him to make *him* feel bad?"

Will drank ginger ale that night and eventually calmed down. When he got home, he read until he got sleepy, but he tossed and turned most of the night. Just before daybreak, he drifted off and had a wild dream of being in Brazil, trying to escape from a jungle that kept changing to a warehouse.

He described it to Blair. "When I woke up, I was so relieved to be at home and not in Brazil that life took on a new meaning. I hadn't cleaned my apartment in weeks, so, I dug out all those cleaning agents I hadn't opened. I started in the morning and cleaned and vacuumed for three hours.

When I was through, the smell of the cleaning agents and the shine of every surface made me feel like a new man.

Blair laughed.

"I showered and then my nose told me that Chichi had brought up one of Rosa's meals. I opened the door, and Cozy was sitting there without even trying to steal the roasted chicken. I let him in and we ate together. He has become my best dinner partner. For the first time, I felt like going to a meeting and, for the first time, staying to the end of a meeting didn't bother me."

CHAPTER 16

Inclinations

The next evening, Will had a private session with Grace. The others in the group had gone to a separate meeting devoted to their special drug issues. He talked openly about his recovery progress.

"It's not easy to look back on some of the messes I got in. Taking inventory is not easy when there's so much water over the dam. It's not hard for me to be sorry, but that feels incomplete when no one is there to hear it. It's too late."

"Some people address those things with a higher power. *Being* sorry is what's important, and of course your willingness to change the behavior that caused harm. When you ask for help, you're admitting your limited power. That's all. It's really that simple, but it must be sincere. Don't get yourself all twisted up over the higher power issue that bothers you so much. Remember, you're asking for help because you alone can't always help yourself out of some situations.

"Don't be so hard on yourself, Will. Learn to love yourself. How can you expect to have compassion for others if you don't have it for yourself?"

She smiled. "You have to love yourself before you can love someone else. You might surprise yourself and fall in love again someday."

He laughed. "I expect to make some improvements, but I don't think that will ever happen. I've met many women since my divorce, but I never fell in love with any of them."

He changed the subject. "I thought about the people I've wronged. It's not such a long list, but making amends is not easy. I'm okay with owning up to things I've done, mostly the trouble I caused Barbara. I just don't know what to do about it now. I can't go up to her now that she's married and say 'I'm sorry.' There's just no opportunity to do that. I have let my mother know how sorry I am to have caused her and my father so much sorrow. But, my father is dead and so I'll never be able to tell him I'm sorry."

Grace offered him a way out. "You can do this even if the person you're addressing is not physically there. This is one of the most difficult steps and also one of the most freeing. It's not easy to confront yourself on this. The ninth step is a little muddy because you don't want to open up wounds that could stir up hard feelings, like with Barbara. Only you can decide if you can broach the past with her. But, an apology straight from the heart goes a long way."

Will shifted "I'm not used to digging up the past and trying to figure myself out psychologically. Only recently did I start loosening up and I think that's because of the diary. It's given me the courage to open up about my feelings. And you . . . I say more about myself in this room than I do with Dr. Worthington. I tell him about events in my life; but I tell you about me."

Grace smiled. "Self-reflection doesn't come easily. You need to bring yourself to a quiet place where the past can surface without causing anger or rage. The mind is a curious thing. Unless we take charge of it, the mind will ramble on and even run us into the ground. Troubling thoughts surface as if they had happened yesterday."

"Yeah, I've done that," Will admitted. "I still feel angry over things that happened twenty years ago. I saw a movie once, called *Buffalo Boy*. There was this wise Chinese man telling his boy not to let habits and inclinations roam free in his mind. He said the only thing that can safely roam free is truth. I hope I never forget that."

"Sounds like something people in the group might enjoy. You spoke of loosening up after reading Faith's diary. That's self-reflection. I'd go with that. Just bring yourself to a quiet place, then let your feelings surface as long as they don't anger you. If you make an honest attempt, something good may happen. Don't be too quick to resurrect something that will enrage you unless you're prepared to handle it."

"Here's something Faith says that really interests me," Will said turning to the diary he had been holding, his thumb still on the page.

My mind easily forms habits and hates giving them up. Bad habits need to be worked on for a lifetime because they are embedded in the circuitry of my mind. They may shadow me for a lifetime. I must learn to keep them benign.

It is difficult to forgive others, but it is even more difficult to forgive myself for my weakness and transgressions. What needs to be forgiven will continue to cause irritation. Genuine forgiveness comes on the heels of compassion. I am in the process of a transformation of feelings. My mind wants to race ahead of my feelings. I must try to keep my balance.

My mind goes in a circle and has limitations. I am able to comprehend one part of the circular structure but I cannot grasp the whole of myself because I cannot think outside myself. No matter how I try, I cannot be an object to myself, only a subject.

I must give up this chicken and egg routine and find another route to the truth. I hold onto troubling thoughts for too long. I must prepare for harder work, and learn to read the signs. Signs come in many forms. There is always a sign when trouble is brewing or when something needs fixing.

"I think the eighth and ninth steps may be too adventurous for someone with my history," Will confessed.

Grace smiled. "When you dig into the past be sure to do so with an open heart. Take stock in the words of the diary. Know your boundaries. Don't let anger flare because that will only feed your anxiety. Feelings are like endless ripples in a stream. They'll flow as long as you let them, so they must be channeled. Anxiety like yours only compounds the addiction problem."

"Mine must be compounded big time."

"It may take a while to bring your anxiety under control. But, you can begin the healing process by learning how to get to a quiet place."

"I guess this is where meditation comes in," Will remarked. "I'm learning to put random thoughts on hold. That's not my strong suit but I find that getting to a quiet place doesn't have to be like a lesson plan. I've been quieted by having my dog, Cozy, beside me. Well, Cozy is not really my dog, but he thinks he is. I try to quiet myself and let go of the thinking process."

"The goal is achieved in various ways," Grace added. "When you visit a wisdom figure, you don't pound at the door demanding to be let in. You approach the door and knock quietly and wait for it to open. That is the way to approach the door inside you, the door that opens to a place bigger than you can imagine. Things you couldn't understand before, you may understand now."

"Like sitting at the feet of the Buddha and waiting," Will added. "I've spent too much time being anxious. I don't want to spend the rest of my life like that. It's not going to be easy. I'm used to keeping baggage to myself."

"Yes. I know," Grace replied. "The baggage you have is yours whether you like it or not. You'll have it the rest of your life, so you must check on it routinely. Go back to the seventh step. Ask yourself, how am I doing with this pack? Am I trying to hand it over to others and make them carry my load when they have burdens of their own? If you lighten your load, you'll relieve yourself of a great burden, and when you do need to hand it over to someone else, as we some-times do out of weakness, the burden we give them won't be too great. Trust me, Will. You can break this cycle of fear and anger in yourself."

CHAPTER 17

Appearance of Being Sober

It was three months since Will began drug therapy with Dr. Worthington and he was still a long way from feeling better. Whenever he slept well there was no accounting for it. He pushed himself to think about working out.

Today, there was banking to be done and he wanted to see Phineas. The phone rang as he was going out the door. It was his friend in Arizona.

"You seemed out of sorts the last time you were here and I thought maybe I could make it better the next time," her voice said invitingly.

In past years, he might have hopped a plane the next day, but he was different now. "You're right about that," he admitted. "I'm sure you noticed that I just wasn't myself. A lot was going on. You did everything to make a good time for both of us."

"It must be pretty ugly up there this time of year. If I remember, March is neither here nor there. Why not come out to Sedona?"

"Thanks for the invitation. There are lots of loose ends here right now."

She wasn't one to push him. "You know you're always welcome. All you have to do is pick up the phone. If I don't hear from you in a few weeks, I'll phone again and try to push harder. Maybe your schedule will ease up by then."

He hung up the phone and looked out at the bleakness of March. *A nothing time of year*, he had to agree, but the desolation he felt inside was worse than the weather outside.

He met with Dr. Worthington. Their relationship was becoming strained and for much of the visit they stared at each other or the floor. He told Worthington that the new medications were not working.

"Maybe you need to be more patient," Worthington replied.

This was not what Will wanted to hear. He was impatient and for good reason. All his life he had been used to getting a quick fix from alcohol and it crossed his mind while sitting across from Worthington that a few shots of Vodka would end the misery. He was frustrated with psychiatry and with AA meetings. He wanted to get back to the way he was . . . just one of the guys at Sonny's.

In his sessions with Dr. Worthington, Will had talked about ordinary events in his life but not his most private feelings. There was something unnatural about it, he thought, and he made an effort to safeguard his privacy. It wasn't that way with Grace. She never seemed to be expecting the revelation of a dark secret. Now he was thinking that maybe he *was* harboring some dark secret after all. Certainly,

Worthington had made him feel that way. The silences during the fifty-minutes were bothersome and Will spent much of the time dodging the openings to say more than he wanted to say.

If he thinks I'm being uncooperative then let him think that. At least I'm sober.

And so he took it amiss when Worthington challenged him about being sober.

"Sobriety may be giving you the false impression of recovery, Will. Sobriety by itself is only part of the process. You need to work on building a self image that is not entirely dependent on will power or the strength of your fist."

Will left the session feeling estranged from Worthington. He wanted things to be as they were when he could sit and talk about his life as he had remembered it, even his experiences in the Army and in bars. Will thought that Worthington had tried to make something out of nothing by drawing a connection between Will's fixed lines of architecture and his unbending view of himself, but fortunately, that notion went no further.

Will stopped to buy cigarettes and to visit with Phineas; he noticed how much his friend had changed since the shooting. The store was busy when he arrived and so he didn't stay long enough to enjoy a brew from the pot Phineas kept going for the better part of the day. On the drive home, Will became aware of the determined sound of the old Volvo motor, and now the hum of tires on macadam drummed out the vexing session with Worthington. He entertained the notion of a higher power and found himself still baffled by it. He had discussed this with Grace on more than one occasion after reading the diary. Now, Faith seemed to him little more than a figment of his imagination, and he was feeling bereft for what might never materialize. The thought occurred to him that after all the energy he had devoted to the higher power matter, he was making no headway. He laughed at himself thinking that even his Volvo was advancing with its wheels spinning.

When he pulled into the driveway, Chichi was already sprinkling salt on the surface in preparation for a late winter storm that would force Will to stay home the rest of the day. He phoned his mother to tell her that he would not be coming for supper. That night, he slept in fits and starts and woke up in a sweat because of another violent dream. When he looked out the window in the morning, snow covered the ground, and he thought about the lonely woman who had picked him up at Sonny's so many years ago and to waking up to snow on Easter.

CHAPTER 18

Sound of Locusts

Will saw Grace on Tuesday. She began the session with a selection of music that transformed the dull room into sounds of the woodland. Will was reluctant to participate, but he closed his eyes and listened to water rushing over stones, a swift-moving river cutting a path downstream where he would very much like to travel. He tried to hold the image but random thoughts kept surfacing and soon he discovered that the quieting process could not be turned on with a toggle switch. When the music ended, others in the group began to talk calmly and openly about problems that had come up during the week. Will didn't have much to say but the images of nature remained with him even on the drive home.

During the night his sleep was interrupted by a nightmare that woke him up at 4:00 a.m. He couldn't get back to sleep and as a result he was tired and agitated all day. In the afternoon, he forced himself to go out to a Big Book meeting. He had read somewhere that the first Alcoholics

Anonymous book of 1939 was printed on such thick paper that it was given the name *big book*.

The speaker was familiar to some of the people in the room but not to Will. Her talk was on the ways alcoholics hold loved ones hostage by their addiction.

She proclaimed, "we alcoholics often unleash our problems when we're drinking but we have a hard time confronting problems in a healthy way when we're sober. What happens when we're sober? Ask yourself if you have fixed any of the problems you engendered over the years. My guess is that many of you are still in denial."

People nodded in agreement, and she drew them in deeper. "Most of us need help after getting sober because we lack the necessary personal and social skills to handle the challenges that await us."

The audience nodded in agreement.

"How many of you wonder why your relationships have not improved since you got sober? It should come as no surprise that sobriety alone doesn't mean we're on the path to recovery. We need support to help us face our problems and make us whole again."

Whole again, Will repeated . . . *not bad*.

Will contained a smirk, thinking that she might have been in touch with Dr. Worthington.

"We need to find ways to manage our problems," she said, advisedly. "Those alcoholic men in 1935 discovered that the road to recovery began when they shared their plight with each other. Something big happens the moment we share our story with someone who is in the same boat with us.

"And speaking of boats, did you like the boat you were in before you got sober?"

The audience issued a resounding "No."

Will was familiar with the speaker's style of keeping the audience on their toes, encouraging them to participate like schoolchildren in want of more.

"Did any of you wake up one day to discover that your spouse had already bailed out of your boat?"

Now they're eating out of her hand, Will thought, hearing the commotion mixed with laughter.

She commiserated with them. "By the time we got sober, many of us had lost everything of value. Many of us believed that sobriety would set things right and even restore our relationships.

"While we were busy drinking, our spouses learned to live without us.

"And guess what?" she added. "Many of them got used to it."

People started clapping, their actions begging her to continue.

"Spouses left and never came back. Some stayed because they wanted to and others stayed because they didn't have the strength to leave. Does that ring a bell with any of you?"

A few people nodded.

"Now, for those of you whose spouses stuck by you, I will ask you to think about how it is for them now. Are you still holding them hostage with your other big weapon: anger?"

The room fell silent again.

"If you haven't addressed your anger or talked about your feelings, you're a long way from recovery."

People shifted in their seats. Will's face flushed when he realized that Worthington's words had somehow found their way into the room.

"We have a difficulty talking about our feelings," she said, emphasizing men in particular. "Recovery is not for wimps! It takes courage to examine ourselves and accept the truth of the persons we were when we were drinking. If an AA meeting is all that's available to you, take advantage of it. Talking about your feelings in a group is better than wrestling with them alone. Remember, if you're sitting on a mountain of anger, expect an explosion. And when that happens, what do we reach for?"

"A drink!" someone yelled.

By now, Will had heard enough, but he had mistakenly seated himself where a quick departure would be noticeable; and so, there he remained with the uncomfortable awareness that the talk was not close to ending.

"Have you ever asked yourself why you're angry?" she asked, not expecting an answer. "What are you so angry about? And, if you have cause to be angry, do you have the right to make others pay for it? Now there's a wimp for you . . . someone who expects others to pay for their anger. Anger should be short-lived; it's not supposed to camp out in us for a lifetime. But the truth is that for some of us, anger is a lifetime habit."

She paced back and forth a few times and people recrossed their legs and adjusted their positions in the seats.

"I can say from experience . . . if you haven't begun to deal with anger, your relationships are in trouble. Anger makes everyone around you a hostage, and who wants to be around an active volcano?"

Will saw that people were laughing but in a serious way. He was nearly desperate to leave the room when the speaker began winding down her talk, and so he stayed for her last remarks.

"We say we want to improve a relationship or build a new relationship. I'd like to offer a few tips to help you get started or to keep you going on this journey. Ask yourself who carries your baggage. If it's not you carrying the load then someone else must be carrying it for you. When you are at the crossroads, always ask for help from a source greater than yourself, not from a source of power as limited as yours. Healthy relationships are not one-sided; they are reciprocal by nature. Face up to your weakness, and don't despair. Keep the faith. There is hope."

Will was the first to leave. The speaker had given a good talk, he thought, but much of it he had heard before. He drove home with the tempting thought that a shot of Vodka would bring him back to the man he knew as Will Valentine; and it occurred to him that keeping that notion alive was like having money in the bank.

That night he dreamed he was getting married in what seemed like an open-air market. Rosa was frying pieces of bread and passing them out to people walking by. There was turmoil as there had been in most of his recent dreams. Will got lost trying to find the way to the altar.

At the end of April a spurt of energy made him feel like working out again. He attributed it to the air, rich with the pungent odor of last year's vegetation. He longed to be part of the new season with sap beginning its course, spring showing itself with the display of rust-colored buds on Maple trees.

Will was taking his medication regularly but now it was making his stomach sick. Every day was much the same, waking at 5:00 a.m. after a night of fury from bad dreams. Except for a short workout session he tried to fill the days with mundane activities until he could be on the sofa with Cozy. He hadn't slept in his bed since he began taking the new medication.

Blair made another trip to South America, and he missed her terribly. She phoned twice from Lima, and that gave him a lift. He never let on that he was hurting, but he figured she probably knew it anyway.

In May, Worthington took him off the medication. He had already gone through two trials and now the list was getting longer. At the end of May, Worthington changed his medication once again.

When Will saw Blair on Memorial Day, she boosted his morale telling him that she could see the change in his body from working out. But his head didn't feel right and he was afraid something bad was happening. The sound of locusts persisted and his ears rang constantly. He continued to meet with Grace.

CHAPTER 19

Depression

All summer, Will hung on by sheer inertia. He went out to the store before the shoppers showed up and went to the Laundromat before 7:00 a.m. Both alcohol and medications had taken a toll on him. Depression was setting in. Even in the worst of times, he had found something to joke about with Blair. But she noticed that his sense of humor was about gone. Alcohol no longer worked for him and medications did no more than cause nightmares. He spent most days in the apartment, afraid to venture out. Cozy stayed close and every so often Chichi would call to him from downstairs and take the little dog out for a pee. Rosa made a hot meal for him all the days that he sat looking out the window at a world slipping away. He was no longer a part of it. Out of desperation, he picked up Faith's diary and re-read the part on depression.

I'm caught by surprise. Depression comes over me like the changing wind and in that instant I am no longer connected to the world. I don't move for fear I'll go down in the darkness. Yesterday, I was free in the wholeness of my being and now I'm a stranger to myself. I am a prisoner in nothingness. What starts this off? What is it that is so powerful it erases all hope from the horizon? I sense myself not as a whole being ~ body, mind, spirit, emotion, but a singular entity acutely conscious, a mind disconnected from the whole of myself and all alone in nothingness. All afternoon I hug the couch in the aftermath of this cataclysm. Yesterday, the sun spread its diamonds across the sea. Today, a demon has brought me to this morbid place that overlooks an empty grave. I have forgotten the purpose of seasons. My psyche is disconnected from its wholeness. I'm enclosed in a vacuum.

All day I lay in this dark cocoon in fear of rankling demons. I pray for a grace that will let me perform one simple act of the will. I keep my eye on my open grave and slowly bring my cup to the sink and wipe the table clean. A bowl of flowers on pure white linen is all that I can muster. I try to remember the words I was taught but my catechism escapes me. I forget the purpose of prayer. I wonder if the sun will come up in the morning.

Will read the words that described Faith's dire situation. She was as bad off as he was and he thought *if she makes it then maybe I can make it but how will I know if I can't find her?* He considered repeating the Lost and Found ad in the newspaper but that seemed ineffectual. He would post a notice at an AA meeting. He needed consolation. Out of desperation, he turned to the Serenity Prayer.

God, grant us the serenity to accept the things we cannot change, the courage to change the things we can, and the wisdom to know the difference.

He thought about wisdom. *To know the difference between what I cannot change and what I can change. How can I change my addiction to alcohol? I don't even know how strong I am or how much courage I have.* Faith's diary was still in his hands. He flipped the pages looking for something more, help really.

The pond is solid ice. Cemetery faucets are frozen. Cars come and go. People drop off pretty flowers, hoping to ward off death. Flowers lay frozen on blue ice. Grieving minds visit the dead but they should not stay too long. They must leave this frozen place and not allow themselves to be entombed while the door to life is still open.

CHAPTER 20

Laura Mackenzie

Summer was over. The new round of medications provided a modicum of relief, enough to be able to sit through part of an AA meeting. Coffee was Will's excuse to get up from the chair whenever he had enough of sitting.

No meeting really suited him until he discovered the meetings at St. Bridget's, which focused on anxiety. As he described it to Blair, "This place is not in my own backyard and the people who go there are in a similar situation. It always helps to be in with a bunch of crazies like myself."

Tonight, the air outside St. Bridget's hall was hot from the September afternoon. The break came just in time for a much needed smoke. The Alanon meeting next door was also breaking and Will stood against the stone wall, watching people gather 'round to talk about the heat of the day.

It had been an hour since the last cigarette and this was the moment to relish. There was that unique way of lighting up—a short puff, a quick exhale of the initial bite. The sec-

ond puff was the real thing, a deep draw carrying the necessary drug to that place inside the chest. Will kept his head
erect and exhaled. The perfect moment connected him to
the world and took less than five seconds. He was a true
Marlboro man.

He propped up his foot against the concrete wall as if to
survey the parking lot, listening to people around him chat-
tering away in small groups. A woman fumbled with a pack
of cigarettes in one hand, trying to feel her way through her
leather bag that looked more like the feeding halter for a
horse. Will reached out and offered her a light. "Is this what
you're looking for?"

She looked up and smiled. "I know it's somewhere at
the bottom of the heap. Thanks."

She exhaled toward the parking lot. "Not much of a
view is it?"

Will would have replied but her friends beckoned
her.

"Thanks for the light," she said, turning away.

He looked toward the door. His eye caught the swish of
a ponytail and for a moment he thought of Blair. He watched
the pretty woman come out onto the terrace and when she
turned toward him, something stirred as if he had recognized an old friend.

"Hot, huh?" he said.

"Ooh!" she exclaimed, her voice on the verge of singing. "Our room has a fan, but on a night like this, there's not
much you can do but be hot."

Anyone watching would guess that they were friends, casually discussing the day while gazing out at the parking lot.

"This is my first meeting," she said. "It's very interesting."

"You're in Alanon?"

"Yes," she said. "I'm trying to understand what my father went through for most of his life. He passed away last year. I'm Laura Mackenzie."

"Will," he said, extending his hand.

"Nice to meet you, Will."

They made small talk and laughed easily; he learned that she was a cardiac nurse at the hospital. They kept their gaze on the neutral zone of the parking lot, as though looking eye to eye might stir something lying below the surface of their smiles. They conversed in a lively manner until the sudden silence on the patio let them know that everyone had gone inside. They walked to the door, reluctant to part.

"Back to live action," Laura remarked.

In a bold move, Will tested the water. "We could go out for coffee, instead."

She looked back at him. "Well, yes, we could, maybe next time."

They smiled, waved each other off and rejoined their meetings.

Will's meeting ended an hour later and he lingered in the parking lot hoping to see the pretty girl with her pony tail glistening in the sunlight. He was sorry he hadn't asked when she would be coming back.

For the next week and a half, he attended as many meetings as possible while keeping an eye out for the woman who had been on his mind since they met. Her name kept repeating in his head like a song that lodges in the brain. *Laura Mackenzie, Laura Mackenzie.*

September nights were starting to cool down. During the break, Will stood on the terrace, looking out over the parking lot while keeping an eye on the door, hoping to see her. He had sat through more meetings than he was used to and his tenacity paid off when he caught a glimpse of her through the double glass doors. It *was* Laura! But a man was at her side and they were laughing as they came out onto the terrace. Will felt embarrassed now for his jealousy that surged out of nowhere, and he cursed himself for allowing a crush to flare into passion. But she waved to the man, and he went off to join a group of people. The weight of the world lifted off Will.

Laura came over to him and they stood together in the same spot where they had met.

"Hi," she said. "Haven't we met before?"

"Hi, Mackenzie," he quipped, wanting her to laugh.

They would do it again, break the ice for the second time, and he tried to take her in all at once. Now he noticed the tiny freckles on her nose, her big green-blue eyes. He was hearing the voice he had been trying to remember, telling him that she hadn't been to an Alanon meeting since that first night because of her work schedule.

He offered her a cigarette, expecting that she didn't smoke, and now he wished he had quit when he felt the impetus to do so a while back.

They took the safe course and talked about the mundane and how much the temperature had cooled down in just two weeks, and then it was time to go inside. They started for the door and Will found the courage to ask her out for the second time. "Would you like to go out for coffee after the meeting?" She looked into his eyes and said that she'd like that very much. Everything changed for Will, as if past and present had suddenly rolled up into one moment of happiness. They agreed to go over to Chet's for ice cream that was homemade and the best in town. He suggested a plan. "My meeting usually gets out a few minutes before yours. I can wait for you. Why not leave your car here, and I'll drive you back later."

"I have an early work day tomorrow," she said. "Maybe it would be better if I just follow you in my car."

"Sure," he said, figuring that she wanted to scope him out a bit. After all he was almost a stranger.

They parted, but not for long. They took to each other so easily that there was no turning back and no slowing down. It was Will and Laura, together every weekend, and by the end of October they were inseparable. November came and Will was spending at least one night a week at Laura's place.

He was almost sorry he had mentioned his enthusiasm to Grace when she advised him to move slowly. Her cautious reminder pissed him off. *The first time all year I have something to look forward to and she goes mother on me.* It was time to tell his sister the good news about Laura.

CHAPTER 21

Telling Blair

He hadn't seen Blair in weeks. He rang the doorbell and watched Castor peering out from the window, his yellow eyes slanting upward, his body language indicating that a friend had arrived.

"Hi stranger!" Blair said, giving her brother the usual bear hug.

"What's cookin'?" he asked. "Sure smells good."

"Roast loin of pork," she replied, taking his jacket.

Castor jumped down from the window seat.

"Come sit at the table. We can talk while I get dinner. It's nearly ready."

"You look terrific," she said. "Happy, even."

"I feel pretty good," he replied, thinking of his news about Laura.

Castor purred on his lap and Blair put dinner on the table.

"Oh boy!" Will exclaimed eyeing the meat, oven-roasted potatoes, and applesauce.

"Please start serving yourself," Blair called out. "I'll get the seltzer."

"Sorry, Castor," Will said, putting the cat on the floor.

"Can't wait to dig in," he said. "I'm starved!"

They were halfway through dinner. He waited for Blair to finish telling him about the experience in South America before breaking the news. "I'm seeing someone."

Blair stopped chewing.

"Omigod, I should have guessed . . . by the way you look. Is that why you haven't phoned me? So tell me."

He began with the basics. "Well, her name is Laura Mackenzie. We met during a break on the terrace of St. Bridget's hall. She was there for an Alanon meeting. Her father was a drinker, a lifer. He died last year. She's a nurse . . . a pretty one!"

Blair flushed with excitement. Will described Laura in detail, without being prompted.

"She has light hair," he said, looking at Blair. ". . . kind of pulls it back the way you do. And yes, I do remember the color of her eyes. They're green, more green than blue."

"Tell me more," Blair said, enjoying her brother's happiness.

"She was married for a few years but that didn't work out. Fortunately for me! She's been divorced for years."

"Kids?" Blair asked.

"No, thank God. I don't think I could handle that," Will remarked laughing. "She's a cardiac nurse at the hospital."

"Does Mom know?"

"No," he said. "Only Grace knows. I figured by now I should say something because the relationship is getting serious. I've been spending a lot of time at her place."

"I suppose you have to watch yourself," Blair remarked, trying not to make it sound like a warning.

"Yeah, I know," he said. "But, it's not like she's in recovery."

"I know. I know," Blair agreed. "It's just that a relationship adds pressure and you have to be strong to handle it."

She was being overly cautious, Will thought, and he went on the offensive.

"Well, if you want the truth, it's too late. We're really hooked on each other. I'm not about to let *her* go."

His admission took Blair by surprised.

"Well, then, there's no turning back."

"No." he admitted.

"Laura knows about the anxiety, right?"

"There's not much I haven't told her. She agrees with me that I should be treated with an anxiety-specific medication. She thinks other things in my life will fall into place if the anxiety is controlled. That's what I think, too. I still haven't found a medication that works without causing side effects. Anything that takes away the anxiety makes me feel sleepy during the day. You can't live a normal life feeling like that."

"No, that's for sure," Blair agreed.

"I've been feeling almost like my old self since meeting Laura. It feels good to have this relationship. And I like . . . well, almost like, the AA meetings at St. Bridget's. I still get a bit hyper when I stay too long. I can deal with that once in a while, but when it persists for a week or two, that's when I think of drinking. Anxiety wears down a person's stamina. Right now, the medication I'm taking helps, but it makes me tired during the day and I don't have the normal . . . you know, energy that I had. I just don't feel like myself."

Will didn't want to come right out with the word *libido* and he wasn't even sure if he would have talked about it further if Blair had asked, but she didn't pick up on it and so he let it go.

"I even tried the St. John's Wort you told me about and for a while I thought it was working. But it all flared up again, so it must have been the placebo effect. No sense taking it. It also causes sun sensitivity."

"Hey . . . so will they be sending you back to South America?" Will asked, meaning to change the subject.

"Not for a good while. I brought something back for you." She took the package from the table.

"It's from Peru," she said, handing him the gift, a hand-carved wooden horse.

"When I saw it, I thought of that horse you said you had when you were a boy, like the one in Monet's painting. I hope you like it."

Will was touched by Blair's gift.

They talked about the political unrest in Peru and the dangers for journalists. Blair assured him that she was always put up in a safe hotel. Her assignment had gone very well, she told him, and she was becoming known in the *fast circles*.

"My boss says I make him look good," she admitted.

"That's what it's all about, making your boss look good," he replied.

They talked more about Laura's job at the hospital, and then Blair asked him how much longer he'd be in therapy with the bronze goddess, as they referred to Grace Manning.

"Not much longer," he told her. "The sessions with her are just about over. I'll be glad to be done with that. I'll have to see Worthington as long as I'm on medication. I might miss seeing Grace but I won't miss Worthington."

Castor and Pollux followed Will to the door.

"You never mentioned what Grace said about your relationship."

"She said plenty," he said, pointing his thumb down.

"Oh, Oh!" she replied. "That's not good."

"She's wary of it because it came so soon in my recovery. I know the dangers of getting emotionally involved but I'm not about to end this relationship. Grace knows her limits. She said, 'It's up to you the way you live your life. I can only point the way with some degree of wisdom.'"

"Well," Blair remarked, "I respect her wisdom, but, I'm glad you met Laura. Maybe this is a good thing. When can I meet her?"

"She asked the same about you. We'll do it soon," he replied. "Real soon."

CHAPTER 22

Sunday Dinner

Laura was at the front door when Will drove up. Pretty, he thought, seeing her in her dark slacks and matching jacket and white collarless blouse. "Don't get out, I'll come around," she said, but Will got out of the car anyway when he saw that she was carrying the gift packages for his mother and daughter.

"Hmm, you smell delicious," he said, taking a deeper breath.

"Can you tell I'm nervous?"

"Yes, it shows on your face. Stop worrying. She's my mother, not the pope."

"I know," she said, forcing a laugh. "But meeting the pope would be easier because he's not your mother. I'm normally easy about meeting people but this feels different."

"Samantha's there," Will said. You'll like her. You look very nice. I like that outfit. So, what did you decide on?"

"I got a bluish gray alpaca shawl for your mother and really pretty earrings for Samantha."

"They'll like that." Will reached for her hand. They arrived at his mother's condominium in the late afternoon. Lydia Valentine greeted them, looking vibrant and youthful in a black turtleneck sweater and gray slacks, and displaying a touch of glamour with her salt and pepper hair fastened on one side with a tortoiseshell barrette. Will had no doubt Laura would be well received but he knew she had passed muster when his mother asked to be called Lydia.

Laura sat down on the sofa next to Will, and Samantha offered them some iced tea, seeming pleased to be helping her grandmother. Laura glanced around the living room and compliment Lydia on her decorating style. Lydia had placed the gifts on the coffee table and now Will said, jokingly, that they should be opened before they got cold. He further commented that Laura had spent an entire week looking for the perfect gifts.

Everyone was delighted with Will's humor which lessoned the tension for Laura. There was no doubt that the gifts were well-chosen when Samantha went over to the large mirror on the wall above the credenza to put on the earrings, and Lydia wrapped the shawl around her shoulders, her smile indicating that she would have chosen it for herself.

The aroma of beef stew caused Samantha to excuse herself and go to the kitchen to stir the pot.

"I thought we'd have an early dinner," Lydia explained. "Samantha has an early morning flight."

Laura listened to pleasant tales about the neighborhood where Will had grown up, and to Samantha's passionate interest in her job at the university. Will sat back and let the women do the talking, watching the people he loved most bond together. His mother surprised him when she told Laura about the sudden and unexpected passing of her husband, Hugh Valentine, and revealed her feeling of guilt that she might have prevented it. Laura spoke compassionately, telling her how common it is for loved ones, particularly a spouse, to feel that they might have prevented a heart attack, and that little can be done without previous signs of a life-threatening condition. Will was swallowed up in emotion by his mother's sudden revelation. Laura's comment had set well with her. They moved on to other topics, and Will detected an easiness in his mother's face that he hadn't seen in a long time.

While Samantha helped her grandmother in the kitchen, Will showed Laura family photos and a wedding photo of Lydia and Hugh Valentine. They dined on beef stew and homemade biscuits, relaxed in each other's company, and Will felt his family coming together for the first time since his divorce.

"Have you met Blair?" Samantha asked Laura.

"Not yet. She's been traveling so much and I guess she's still catching up on paper work. But, I'm looking forward to meeting her. Maybe next week, right Will?" He nodded. Blair did have paper work to do but she had wisely mentioned to Will that the initial meeting with Laura should be kept simple.

"You'll like her," Samantha remarked. "She's really cool."

"I hear that from your dad all the time," Laura replied.

The meal ended with Lydia's apple cobbler, and soon it was time for Samantha to return to her mother's house. She kissed her father good-bye, and he slipped her some cash and told her to keep away from the boys.

Samantha giggled the way she did when she was a girl, and she turned to Laura. "He's been telling me that since I was twelve. If I keep taking his advice, I'll end up an old maid."

"Say hello to Mom," Will said.

Lydia handed Samantha a package. "Give this to Mom. She loves my cobbler."

When it was time for Will and Laura to leave, Lydia walked them to the elevator where she embraced Laura. They would see each other again, Will knew.

The elevator door closed. "No wonder you're like you are, Will Valentine. You have a beautiful family. You look like your mother, especially the eyes. Samantha's hair is lighter than it looked in the photo you showed me."

"Yeah, she has her mother's hair and Valentine eyes. Now, that wasn't so bad, was it?"

"I really got myself worked up for nothing," Laura said, cozying up to Will's body. "She really likes the shawl."

CHAPTER 23

The Urge

Will phoned Frank Sasso to set the starting date for working full-time. Frank praised his design for the Alzheimer's wing and invited him to attend the groundbreaking ceremony. "Please come with Laura," Frank said. "I'd like to meet her. You tell me when you can start."

Will took the prudent course. "How about a month from now, Frank?"

Will should have been flying high but something was troubling him, a personal matter he could not discuss with anyone. He felt certain it was the medication but the possibility that it wasn't scared him. *This is not me*, he thought. Diminished libido was for old men and now the vulgar expression of being unable to get the pecker up kept going through his head, only now it wasn't funny. He had read something about libido in the contraindications of his medication. The only way to be sure would be to test it out, and so he stopped taking the medication, fully aware that it was a bad choice. In a week's time his sexual energy returned. The downside was that his anxiety flared up again.

It would take more than being in love and having a job to feel whole again. His love for Laura was growing richer and now their future together meant everything to him. Always the question—*why the anxiety when everything good is happening*. One slip with alcohol would bring him down again and now the fear of losing Laura weighed heavily on him.

The urge to drink played on his mind. Out of desperation, he got in touch with the alcohol and addiction center at the V.A. hospital where he had gone through de-tox the previous year. The woman there heard the distressed sound in his voice.

"If you need to talk to someone I can put you in touch with a counselor. Otherwise, there's an open slot on Monday."

The wheels were turning. "I think I can make it through the weekend," he told her. "I'll take that appointment on Monday."

"If you change your mind, call back. Don't try to tough it out."

She instructed him further. "You'll be having blood work that day. Don't have anything to eat or drink after midnight the night before. We'll have coffee for you afterward and maybe a doughnut if there's one left."

"Sounds like pretty good service," he replied, laughing. "Are you sure this is the V.A.?"

The woman chuckled and then went on to say that he would be meeting with a specialist in alcohol related problems. "Plan to be here for a couple of hours."

Will hung up the phone. He was sweating over the close call that in moments might have caused him to lose everything. He stayed close to Laura.

On Monday morning, he drove to the V.A. where a receptionist handed him some paper work to fill out and told him where to go for blood work. Later, he met with a physician who examined him and told him that, for someone who had abused his body for so many years, he was in excellent condition. He had heard that again and again. The doctor listened to Will's pathetic account and said that he had treated hundreds of men in similar situations.

Later, Will met with the addiction counselor. Right off, she was easy to like and he hoped she would be a good listener, as he was about to deliver a running account of failed attempts to relieve his worsening condition.

"Since I started out in the program, I've been asking for relief from anxiety. I probably didn't work the twelve steps as thoroughly as everyone wanted, but I did the best I could under the circumstances. I went through hell a hundred times. Now, I have a wonderful woman in my life. I have a full time job waiting for me. And yet, after all this time, I keep hearing the same story from everyone associated with the recovery program—that a specific anxiety medication could become addictive and therefore no one will prescribe it. This is like one-size-fits-all for everyone who comes through the door."

The woman remained still and didn't attempt to interrupt him.

"I've attended meetings and listened to story after story from recovering alcoholics."

Now, the woman folded and unfolded her hands but she remained quiet.

"I can't spend the rest of my life feeling the way I do. I have a creative life inside me. I'm a damn good architect and I want to go back to work in my profession. No amount of counseling seems to do my anxiety any good. I need a medication even if it's possibly addictive. I'm willing to take that chance. It's certainly better than what I have now."

Will took a breath and that gave her an opening to respond. "We've considered your case. We can give you an anxiety medication for a short period of time, a four-day supply, just to get you through this crisis and hopefully interrupt the cycle."

She wasn't about to waver. *Back to square one*, he thought, *another go 'round for the guinea pig.* There was no other option but to take the four day supply and benefit from a temporary reprieve.

"Take the medication as directed. You can start by taking two capsules before dinner."

He left with trepidations. So far there was no real solution for his dilemma; but he would take the medication as directed if only to break the cycle of anxiety and give him time to re-think the situation.

He went to Laura's in the late afternoon. She had just come in from work.

"Hey, good timing," she called out.

Will told her that Blair had left a message. "David is in from California and she wants to know if we'd meet them tonight for dinner."

"Yes," Laura was quick to reply. "I'm sure she wants you to meet the guy. And that means I don't have to cook. Why not phone her and say we're on for tonight . . . then tell me about your appointment."

Blair picked up Will's call right away. "I was thinking of Gaucho's," she said, laughing. "David's in the mood for red meat. He says he's tired of eating healthy. We'll get a table for six-thirty and wait for you."

"She's happy," Will said to Laura when he got off the phone. "I can hear it in her voice."

Laura listened with dismay to Will's account of the experience at the V.A., but she wasn't one to cave from the disappointment. Together they decided to make the best of the short-term break in the cycle of anxiety and come up with a new plan.

"Here goes," Will said, before swallowing two capsules.

When they arrived at Gaucho's, Blair and David were already seated. The crowd was buzzing, and lively Brazilian music played in the background. Most of the seats at the bar were filled. Will noticed the long-stemmed Martini glasses filled with new concoctions favored by the younger set.

Blair made the introductions and proceeded to talk non-stop as if the success of the evening depended on her. Will assessed David as a dyed in the wool California type, perhaps by the cut of his hair and a vibrant complexion that people on the east coast weren't used to seeing except in summer; he had no expectations that his sister's relationship with David would cause her to move to the west coast. Eventually, Blair settled down and David was able to talk about the financial group he was in. Listening, Will felt that the man was an okay kind of guy.

David seemed genuinely interested in architectural design and Will was just getting into it when the sick feeling came over him. He strained to stay on track with their conversation. At first his stomach felt a little queasy but then the nausea persisted until he could no longer remain at the table.

Laura noticed his face perspiring and then turn the color of putty. "Are are you okay?" she asked.

"Excuse me," he mumbled into his napkin, and then hurried to the men's room.

When he returned to the table, Will apologized and said that he couldn't stay for dinner. Laura helped him make a quick departure. The cool air outdoors helped the feeling but he needed to get home. "Drive fast. I'm feeling sick to my stomach. I hope I can make it."

They drove with the window open until he could no longer contain himself and Laura pulled the car over to the side of the road just in time. The new medication that had been their hope was not one he could tolerate.

CHAPTER 24

Dr. Chan

Laura and Will moved into their newly rented condo. Blair remarked to her mother that their spirits were high as a hot-air balloon. The physical work of the move helped Will's anxiety, giving him a break he desperately needed. It was not easy to say good-bye to Chichi and Rosa. They had been like a second family when he needed comfort. Will hired a van, and he let Chichi help with the move by carrying a few cartons to the vehicle that were light enough for an old man. Cozy ran up and down the stairs following on Will's heels just the way he did on the day Will moved in. Finally, there was room for only one more box.

"Manicotti," Rosa said. "Thirty minutes in the oven." And then it was time to leave.

Chichi and Rosa stood in the driveway with Cozy at their feet and watched Will drive off. Will looked back at them in the rearview mirror seeing Rosa with her hands on her hips and Chichi waving his handkerchief into the air as if he were calling for help. Will had promised them he'd return to help Chichi plant the garden for the new season and maybe even spend an afternoon at the Italian Club playing cards with Chichi and Bocci Luigi.

There was more than manicotti in the box Rosa gave them, as Laura discovered when she opened the lid and found sausage and peppers, a loaf of Italian bread and angel wings. They vowed that when they were settled they would come back to the south end on Saturday mornings and stock up for the week.

The aroma of Laura's freshly brewed coffee awakened Will and he wasted no time getting out of bed. The moment he put the warm cloth to his face his mind became clear and he knew what he had to do. He was tired of running through the minefield of prescription drugs with little hope for a treatment plan that worked. He had exhausted his patience. There was nothing to lose by taking matters into his hands.

He found the list of physicians in the yellow pages and stopped at the name, Chan. He waited until 9:00 a.m. to dial the number. He was connected after a few redials. When the receptionist offered him an appointment the next day, Will wondered whether he'd made a mistake, but she explained that someone had cancelled last minute and he was the lucky one to fill that slot. There would be no turning back, he promised himself, so he took the appointment that was offered.

The next morning, he waited for Laura to leave for work. She had encouraged him to seek another opinion regarding his medication, but there was no point telling her about the appointment. She'd know soon enough, and why get her hopes up unnecessarily.

When he met Dr. Chan, he couldn't help chuckle to himself finding her to be built like a child, though he figured her to be in her mid forties. She spoke in a clipped Asian manner, occasionally leaving off articles of grammar, and she wasted no time recording a history of his anxiety. He revealed nothing about his being in recovery, though he let her know that he wasn't using alcohol. There was no reason to divulge details of his addiction history. He would wait and see what she prescribed, and if that turned out to be a drug he had already used, then he would tell her more about his prescription medication history. Dr. Chan was more interested in the manifestation of his anxiety than the cause. At one point she offered a slim but genuine smile and said, "jittery not good."

He was expecting resistance, and so he was flabbergasted when Dr. Chan offered him a prescription with a word of confidence that it should work for him. She added that the medication needed careful monitoring, but that was of no concern to him.

"No alcohol," she emphasized, and he laughed to himself thinking that at any minute the cold-turkey community would burst through the door and put him in chains.

She handed him the prescription with the understanding that he would be required to come in for a checkup every six weeks to obtain a refill. That was the deal. If he took the medication as directed and did well on it she would renew the prescription at appropriate intervals. Will detected in her face that she knew more about him than what he had told her. Maybe she was taking a chance on him, but they left it at that, and he was out in the parking lot in less than forty-five minutes.

He had the prescription filled and took the medication as soon as he got home. In half an hour he began to feel different, quieted inside. Maybe it's wishful thinking, he feared. But the feeling persisted well beyond an hour and it felt so good that he prayed it would last. He did some vacuuming and went to the market and shopped for dinner.

Laura came home and saw the table set for dinner and bright red tulips in the vase.

"Hey. What's the occasion?"

"The occasion is that I went to see a new doctor today and the anxiety medication she prescribed made me feel better than I've been in a long time."

Life moved on. There was purpose to his days and he had hope for the future. He had a meaningful AA group at St. Bridget's and a doctor who had listened to him. Dr. Chan had radically changed his life. *The rest is up to me*, he thought. For the first time in his adult life, he wasn't drinking alcohol and he wasn't frozen in anxiety. He was ready to start the full time position at Sasso & Fern.

CHAPTER 25

Faith's Dream

On the way over to Grace's, Will decided not to reveal the name of the doctor he had seen, only that he was trying out a new medication. There were other things he wanted to tell her . . . about the progress he'd made and the stumbling blocks still in front of him.

"It was the sudden urge that always got me," he admitted to Grace. "It would come over me quick as lightening. When addiction really takes hold of a person the desire probably never really goes away entirely. If I let down my guard, it'll get me. I never understood why you were so against my morning visits to Sonny's. I figured, all I was doing was sipping coffee and reading the newspaper. I couldn't see or didn't want to see the danger in that. I believed so much in will power. Now, I know why we're called alcoholics . . . you were right when you said that all the king's horses and all the king's men can't do it for me. I must take control of my addiction and that means keeping away from all the paths leading to danger.

"Desire is always there, lurking in the background . . . a constant. It's up to me to avoid putting a flame to my desire and inviting the urge to take me down.

Grace was about to say something but Will kept talking.

"But, that's not the whole of it. In my case, anxiety is as much of a threat as alcohol. Even if I keep out of Sonny's for the rest of my life I may get the urge to drink if I feel anxiety. That's why I must keep it under control. I'm hoping that this medication will continue to work for me."

Again, Grace was about to say something but he quickly jumped in. "I know . . . I know, you would say that I'm not working the steps the way I should."

She said nothing and let him go on.

"True . . . I have a habit of believing too strongly in my will power. But, I still believe that anxiety is a thing in itself that must be treated. If anxiety returned, I'd be living on the knife's edge, just as I was when I first came here."

"I don't disagree with you about the danger of anxiety," Grace said, getting a word in. "It's just that we hold different views on how it should be treated. It's not just a matter of taking medication. Other supports are important, like going to meetings and opening up with others who suffer, and remembering to use relaxation techniques."

Will wasn't about to argue the matter, not after spending a year trying to get his point across. Instead, he went on to something else.

"I read something interesting in Faith's diary. I'd like to read it to you."

"Sure," Grace said. "Please do."

He opened the diary and read from it:

Last night I dreamed of arriving at a palace gate and walking down a long sunny path leading to a massive entrance door. I'd never been there before but the place felt as familiar as anything I knew. There was a garden along the walkway. Tall stalks with large parchment leaves bent over the walk edge, looking like old people who are just tired of living. I sat for awhile on a stoop, dazzled by the sun. I wanted to knock on the door but I stayed seated instead, feeling the intensity of being in the nexus of something vital. I was at one with the world, with infinite possibilities. I awoke from my dream, thinking that a knock on the door would have changed everything.

"That's it," Will said.

Grace seemed to be expecting more and it took her a few seconds to speak. "I can see why the diary is so important to you. What do you think Faith means when she says that a knock on the door would have changed everything?"

"I think she means that there are moments we should savor, moments that should not be disregarded. Everything we do in life presents us with a choice, an acceptance or a rejection, a knock on the door or the closing of the door. Everything we do has consequences, good or bad. Had I turned away from your door when I came here for my first meeting . . . well, that would have changed everything. It takes wisdom to know whether to open a door or not open it; it takes courage to actually open it or leave it closed."

He kept his finger on the page and continued reading.

"There were times when I thought Faith wasn't going to make it. I mean, she really hit bottom. But, now I think she'll make it. After sifting through the rubble, she deserves the gem she found. All that imagery about the cemetery . . . at first I thought it was morbid, you know, like she was about to end her life or just die from alcoholism. She was always referring to the frozen state, the hard core of a person that cannot budge out of suffering, the embedded turquoise gem, frozen or wedged at the bottom of a river.

"Now, I see the gem as a symbol . . . of her worth and mine. It can be retrieved but it takes courage to melt the ice that imprisons it. Nothing can happen unless the gem dislodges. She ventures out on what she calls a shard of light and explores the mystery, but then she retreats out of fear. She ventures out again, and this time she stays long enough to be touched by the unknown. She knows that she's known! The turquoise gem budges free and life begins. She was virtually dead but she came alive. Her final entry tells what it's like to let go of ego. It looks like a death. It's not a real death but a symbolic death; one that's necessary if she's to go on. Now I understand why the first three steps are still so difficult for me.

"She has no fear as gravediggers dig her symbolic grave because she has already let go of her ego. The grave is dug but it will never contain her, not her essence, the person she is. And neither is ego the essence of a person. When ego is allowed to reign supreme it keeps us from attaining something better. Faith virtually turns herself in and submits to a greater power.

"I wish I could turn myself in, as she did. For me, ego is still what defines me, even though I know that it has no substance. I still use it occasionally as a divining rod to find myself when I'm lost. Maybe in time I'll give up doing that. Faith and I are like the Gemini twins; she being the star of greater magnitude."

CHAPTER 26

Saying Good-Bye

Laura's shift at the hospital began at 7:00 a.m. Will's job was flexible, but they both arose early. Laura was focused on the newspaper on Monday morning when Will came into the kitchen and planted a kiss on her head. He was upbeat about the surprise he had for her.

"How about if I make dinner reservations for Saturday, just the two of us."

Laura was agreeable.

"Sounds good to me. And how about if I pour your coffee."

"Sure," he said. "The aroma is extra good this morning."

"There's something in the paper you should read, in the obituary," she said, handing him the newspaper.

Will looked at the notice that Laura pointed to, and Sonny's name leaped out at him. Stunned, he sat down to read Sonny's death notice.

"He was only forty-seven years old," Laura remarked. "I always pictured him older than that. I never imagined him married with three children. I thought he was just, well . . . I don't know."

"No," he said, gazing past her. "Sonny was quiet, a family man."

She sat down next to him, listening as he talked about Sonny.

"He wouldn't even drink with you if you asked him. I think he drank maybe when he was younger, but he only sipped club soda or ginger ale behind the bar. Whenever a guy wanted him to drink, Sonny always held up his glass containing a soft drink, saying, 'This is what keeps me going all night.'

"No one ever pushed him on that. Sonny didn't talk much, but he had rules in his bar and he kept to them. He didn't go looking for trouble. In all the years, there was only one guy he couldn't handle and I took care of that for him. I'll tell you about it sometime. He kept his place respectable, and he had a way of making everyone feel comfortable."

Will's eyes were fixed on the obituary, but memories suddenly brought to mind a landscape he knew so well—men laughing, the smell of vodka on their cold breath, neon lights reflecting on Christmas snow inching up in front of Sonny's bar and casting a magic spell. These were the nights that were filled with life and light that could only live on in dreams, without their sorrows ruining everything. He looked up at Laura. "The wake is tomorrow, the funeral on Friday. He'll be buried where I played softball, you know, not far from where I grew up."

Laura stood behind him, her hands resting on his shoulders. Will was grappling with the news. "I'm sorry you lost your friend," she said.

Will was so lost in reverie he didn't hear Laura say that she would be getting dressed and that she would see him before leaving for work. The room had turned quiet. He thought back to a few months past when he was at Sonny's, sipping coffee and working on the crossword puzzle. Sonny had seemed in a hurry. "Hey, Will," he said, "I have a doctor's appointment. If you leave before I return, just lock up." Sonny closed the door without even waiting for a reply.

How strange life goes, Will thought—no way he could have known it would be the last time he'd ever see Sonny alive, no way to know which day would be the last day for anybody, for that matter. Life just ends, he thought, without notice or fanfare.

The parking lot of the funeral home was filled when Will got there, and the line of mourners extended down the street and around the block. Will parked his car and came up to the line and stood there listening to people in front of him talking in quiet tones reserved for such occasions, as though Fate had dealt its blow but that they had survived. Will recognized some people up ahead and he nodded when they turned and made eye contact with him.

The raw smell leaching out from the cold earth hadn't changed since the days when he played ball, and despite his sadness over Sonny, he was glad that the baseball season would soon be underway. The line of people advanced slowly. Will turned his head away from the street to avoid the noxious fumes from passing vehicles.

He inched his way into the funeral home where the heavy air seemed depleted of oxygen and laced with the cloying scent of carnations. He signed the guest book and eyed the room, recognizing a few friends and acquaintances. When the man ahead of him stepped forward, Sonny's casket came into view. At first glance, Sonny looked like a man sleeping, but, close-up, the lifeless form of his once vibrant friend was the reality. When it was Will's turn, he stood before the casket and silently said good-bye to the man who was his friend, who provided a home away from home to many sorry-assed men, day and night pouring their booze and listening to their bullshit.

Sonny's wife stood off to the side with the group of mourners. He had seen her on occasion when she came into the bar to discuss a personal matter with Sonny.

"I'm very sorry," Will said, and she reached for his hand as if it were a precious gift. She was gracious, telling Will how appreciative Sonny was of his trust when he left the bar in his hands from time to time.

Will let her know he'd been on the wagon and that he hadn't been at the bar in quite a while. "The last time I saw him he seemed fine," Will offered. "It was early one morning, before he opened up officially. I was having coffee and reading the paper. He said he had to keep a doctor's appointment and asked me if I'd keep an eye on things. I left soon after he returned, and I never saw him again."

Sonny's wife continued holding his hand, and Will thought perhaps she wanted him to say more, as if talking might stave off the bitter loss even for a moment.

"The doctor told him to slow down," she said beseechingly, her brows drawn together, "but he wouldn't change. He was a worrier, about the business and about his family. Now it's too late."

She introduced Will to her two children as a special friend to their father. He shook their hands and offered the only consolation he knew to be true, "Your father always referred to his children as his pride and joy."

When he reached the end of the line of mourners, Will made his way past the wooden chairs and to the rear of the parlor where sofas and upholstered furniture lined the wall. He visited a while with some friends and then left the funeral home with mixed emotions, saddened over the loss of Sonny; glad that he had stopped going to the bar when he did.

The funeral the next morning brought Will back to the cemetery he knew so well. Sonny's grave was located in a section of land that extended far beyond the land where he had played softball. The cemetery looked different to him now because all the land had been used. So long ago, he had memorized the names on each marker and gravestone, but now granite stones went beyond the flat land and stood far out onto the promontory, and he imagined them as the skyline of a city. *What would Sonny think*, he wondered—being laid to rest on the land that held the spirit of get-up games they talked about when no one else was in the bar. They were both Yankee fans. They had spent many happy times together talking about baseball trades made each season, anticipating the day when pitchers and catchers would report.

Will joined the crowd gathering at the gravesite. The scene brought to mind the uneasiness of sitting that close to his father's grave not many years before; his mother, broken-hearted over the loss of her dear Hugh. Now, Sonny's wife was sitting in that chair, close to her dead husband, whose warm hand she held only two days ago. Why such a thing, he wondered—the lure to love in the first place, only to have it taken away in pain and suffering. He thought of his younger days when life was too powerful to be shaken by death. He wasn't one to dwell on such matters but the diary had changed him. Faith wrote about the never-ending cycle of life. Now he stood at the gravesite, feeling himself at the crossroads.

There were prayers of consolation, words meant to take the sting out of the family's desolation and grief. There was hope, after all, in the message that they would see Sonny again in the afterlife, something sweet to satisfy the heart; and oddly enough, Will thought of the plate of sweet buns he had eaten that morning with his coffee. His eyes moved from grave to grave and to the antiquated gray metal faucets, leaning precariously. Cold clear water had flowed from those spigots when old Mike, the caretaker, stood watch over kids in the neighborhood and gave them permission to slurp water after playing ball on the hottest days of summer. This was Mike's cemetery, they had believed. Will pictured him now, silver hair, red-faced and spare, always dressed in grey trousers and a gray shirt; the proprietor of the cemetery who set rules that no one would break. Will had almost forgotten how Mike had sipped something from a small flat bottle he kept in his pocket; now, he realized that it must have been whiskey and he wondered if the man had been more fragile than old.

After the last prayer was recited, mourners walked to their cars in silence, their heads down. All that could be heard was the sound of car doors closing and an occasional "see you over there." Will turned on the motor and drove away, slowly. He caught sight of nearly camouflaged gravediggers kneeling behind the shrubs, their shovels propped up for a morning's work.

Will had decided earlier not to attend the luncheon. Instead, he drove to his office at Sasso & Fern. The finality of Sonny's death hit him harder the farther he got from the cemetery. He had long since stopped going to the bar. Now, with Sonny's death, he was grateful that the decision had been entirely his own and not a consequence of losing Sonny. A chapter in his life had come to an end.

CHAPTER 27

A Ring

Will was delighted with his office, even flabbergasted. He stood with his hands on his hips, then walked around the room, admiring the desktop and drawing board ideally suited for an architect. Frank Sasso came down the hall and stopped at the doorway. "I thought I heard someone. Good to see you, Will."

They shook hands, giving each other a solid grasp of friendship that meant so much to both of them. Frank was a handsome man, tall and nicely built. His intense brown eyes had matched the color of his hair until only recently, when flecks of silver seemed to crop up overnight, making him look the part of the distinguished senior member of Sasso & Fern.

"What do you think of it?" Frank asked, gesturing with his outstretched hands.

Will moved his head from side to side in speechless wonderment. "This is more than I had expected, Frank. I didn't realize you had so much in mind when you said you were refurbishing my office. I can't thank you enough."

They talked about upcoming projects and Will's start date, and then Frank returned to his office. Will sat at his desk and looked around. The painted walls and new wood floor cast a soft warm glow. He phoned the jewelry store and then he called Blair to tell her about the office renovation and to let her know that he'd be picking up the ring on Saturday morning.

"Does she suspect anything?" Blair asked.

"No, I'm sure of it. I made seven-thirty reservations at Lakeside. She thinks it's just the two of us."

"I'll pick up Mom," Blair said. "Samantha called. You know she won't be coming, but she said to tell you that she'll call on Sunday."

"What do you hear from David? Has it turned serious?"

"I don't know," Blair replied. "We talk about being a real couple and living together. He says he wants me to come out there, but I'm afraid that would be a mistake. I love my job in Boston and I'll never be a Californian. We have a great time seeing each other in spurts but who knows what it would be like on a daily basis. I'm going low and slow. Now I know how old maids get to be old maids."

Will laughed. "I knew a lot of young maids who would have been wiser to become old maids."

The following evening Laura and Will stopped at Chet's for ice cream.

"It's such a beautiful evening," she said, "Let's take the long way home."

They drove down the winding country road that recently had been paved. The tires hummed on the surface with the buoyancy of whipped cream. They held hands as lovers do and talked about how rich their lives had become since they met. The more Laura chirped on about how well-suited they were, the easier Will felt about giving her the ring—not that he feared being rejected, but there was a vulnerability to being in such a position, virtually on his knees.

They watched the last two innings of a softball practice game played by high-spirited men past their prime of youth and noticeably out of shape from months of inactivity.

"They need to shed a few pounds," Laura remarked.

Will agreed. "I couldn't help thinking about baseball when I was in line for Sonny's wake—funny what goes through your head even when something serious is going on. We played beer games, mostly. Now, I'd probably run out of steam before reaching first base."

Will regretted that Laura hadn't seen him play ball when he was young and fit, and for a brief second he felt tugged by the reality that it might take them twenty years to discover each other's mysteries.

"I sure enjoyed those games, but I wouldn't want to go back to those nights when I stayed too long in the bar. You wouldn't have wanted to be with me then."

"Well, I'd have liked you, but I'm so glad we met when we did. The time was right for both of us."

When the game ended, they walked hand-in-hand across the grassy lot where they had parked the car, listening to the beer talk getting underway.

"Most of them will stop off for one or two beers before going home. Some of the single guys and the losers will stay until the bar closes."

"It doesn't last long, does it?" She said.

"What's that?"

"Youth," she replied.

"It lasts just long enough to cause a whole lot of trouble," Will said, laughing.

Laura waxed philosophical. "Youth is everything when you're living it because you believe it *is* everything. Looking back, you realize how blind we were with that myopia. Later, when the blinders come off we get to see a wider landscape."

They drove home feeling well about themselves, confident of their future together.

On Saturday morning, Will mentioned to Laura over coffee that he had some errands to do. She wasn't one to question him about niggling matters, and so he left without having to make up a story about where he was going, exactly.

He parked in front of the jewelry store and waited a few minutes until the business was up and running. The clerk, recognizing Will, greeted him with cordial remarks of the day, and said he would bring forth the ring. Will waited patiently, and in a few moments Laura's engagement ring was displayed for him on the black velvet cloth. It was just what he wanted for her, a flawless diamond, beautifully cut.

He would give her the ring that evening, before going to the restaurant. He felt jubilation when he left the store with the tiny box, boyishly innocent, and he understood why people in love must shout their joy to the world.

Will drove over to Newberry's Variety almost feeling the ring burning a hole in his pocket, thinking that he should have planned the morning differently so that he could go directly home after getting the ring. But, this was an important stop, as he was nearly done with his next to last pack of cigarettes and, as he had promised himself, he would smoke one more pack and then quit. He had made the big decision. The thought had been in his mind for most of the year and now he was acting on it. When he drew close to Newberry's Variety store he was stunned seeing the going-out-of-business sign in the window. He pulled over to the curb and read the personal note from Phineas, thanking his loyal customers and friends of fifty years. *Out of business!* Will said aloud, angry that robbers and the recent shooting had caused Phineas to close his store. Phineas had put up a good front, but it was apparent that he had not recovered from the incident that left a man dead only yards from his front door.

Will watched the young newspaper photographer clicking shots of the storefront that was now part of the city's history. He decided not to buy that last pack of cigarettes after all. He was ready to quit anyway, so why not quit in honor of Phineas.

On Saturday evening, Will called out to Laura in their bedroom, as they were dressing for dinner. "Hey, take a look at this."

She finished inserting her earring and came into the bedroom adjusting the little black dress Will loved so much.

"You called?" she quipped from across the room, expecting to be asked about his choice of tie.

Immediately, she caught sight of the little box Will had placed on the bedcover, and she squinted to get a better look. "What's this?" She asked quizzically.

The size and shape of the box pretty much revealed the mystery of what was inside, but the unexpectedness of Will's presentation caused her face to flush, and her failed words caused a virtual traffic jam in her mouth. She looked at him; drew a breath and ran her tongue over her teeth the way she did whenever she had too little time to think things through.

"Go ahead, silly, open it," he said.

They sat together on the bed. Laura ran her fingers over the sides of the stubby box before raising the lid. She gazed at the solitary gem, mesmerized by its beauty. For the moment, Will couldn't discern whether she was enthralled or disappointed but then Laura looked into his eyes and he saw how happy she was.

"Omigod, you caught me by surprise. I had no idea."

Will had anguished over this moment, but now Laura's soft smile assured him that he had made the right move and that it was safe to pop the question.

"Marry me," he said, asking with his eyes.

She kissed his warm cheek, and lingered there.

"Yes, I'll marry you," she said, "if you'll marry me."

"Do you really like it? We can change it." he said.

"Oh, Will. I love it! The solitaire is my favorite, and with these little diamonds on the side. It's perfect and so are you."

"Well, that may be a slight exaggeration," he remarked. "Now you know why we're going to Lakeside. Tonight's special."

He became playful with the sudden relief from tension. "I decided to ask you to marry me *before* we left for Lakeside so in case you said no I could cancel the reservation."

On the drive to the restaurant, Laura turned her hand this way and that to see the light reflecting in the facets of the diamond.

"It's perfect," she kept saying. "I can't believe it's mine. I can't wait to tell Blair. Does she know? Does your mom know? Samantha?"

"Yeah, they all know," he said, his blue eyes glinting.

She interrupted her joy to tell him about the message that had come in that afternoon.

"Frank Sasso called to tell you that a date has been fixed for the celebration of the opening of the new wing for the convalescent home. He asked if you'd phone him on Monday.

"You're coming with me, right?"

"Of course, Mr. Valentine, now that we're a *real* couple I'd be happy to accompany you."

They walked hand and hand across the parking lot, Laura hardly able to take her eyes off the ring, Will looking around for Blair and his mother.

CHAPTER 28

Facing the Truth

On Monday Will told Laura that he would be going to St. Bridget's in the evening for the seven o'clock meeting. The excitement of the weekend had stirred his anxiety and he wasn't about to let it get out of hand. He had thought about his visit to Sedona so long ago and of the worrisome feeling that had come over him at the time—knowing he would drink again, not then, but on a day when he needed to. Since then, he had experienced that feeling more than once, even after he had stabilized his anxiety; but he had not shared this with Laura. Now he was afraid to tell her because they were a committed couple and enjoying a wonderful life together. He was afraid that even Laura, who had attended numerous Alanon meetings, would not understand the sleeping giant that would always be living inside him.

He tried to reason out the cause and effect, hoping to discern what it was that had initiated his desire and signaled an urge to drink that he couldn't turn down. He once admitted to Blair that nothing compared to the feeling he got from alcohol. Now he feared that the desire would remain with him all his life, even with anxiety under control. Maybe his brain was wired to remember the benefit of alcohol but not the history of the fallout.

Blair had challenged him and Laura might do the same, he feared.

"If you feel it coming over you, why do you not contact an AA friend right away, before it takes you over?" Blair had reasoned. "You admit that you get fair warning before the urge gets out of control."

"It's complicated," Will had told her. "It has nothing to do with logic, so if you're thinking along those lines you'll be spinning your wheels.

"There are many levels of this goddamn affliction," he tried to explain. "Taste is one of them, but most of all, it's that wonderful feeling of setting out on the journey to a place where the raw edges of life take a back seat. The journey begins even before that first sip; it's sans souci, not a care in the world."

Blair tried to understand her brother when he described the anticipation of the journey that freed his spirit. "It's like sailing off without boundaries—yourself the boat. It doesn't matter that the journey is short-lived because you don't allow that thought to enter your mind. Problems don't go away; but they just don't bother you for the time you're *out there*. I think that's why I feel relief come over me the moment I give in to the urge; even if I wait a couple of weeks before starting. Looking forward to it makes me feel hopeful and free. Can you understand why at that moment I would *never* go for help?" he pleaded. "Does that make any sense?"

"Then, what you're saying is that at the most critical moment you don't fight against the desire and instead allow it to reach its logical conclusion. All your so-called will power lets you down when you need it most," Blair said, remonstrating with him as he now recalled.

He reflected on that conversation with Blair and it became clear that he still hadn't admitted the truth to himself. *You crazy bastard! You got sober but you can't say you want to stop drinking. Alcohol gave up on you; but in your heart, you didn't give up on alcohol. You still close your eyes and ears even when the freight train is coming straight at you.*

Will was not a fool. He would have to tell Laura about the dangers that lay ahead, but today was not the day.

CHAPTER 29

St. Bridget's

St. Bridget's was especially active on Monday night. Will stood in line for coffee and turned to hear what the guy behind him was saying.

"Looks like people had too much excitement on the weekend," he said, expecting Will to laugh. "I guess that's our speaker back there," he added, pointing to the petite woman engaged in conversation with the people around her.

Will glanced over at the woman, in her fifties, perhaps, youthful looking in jeans and a handsome jacket worn over a colorful blouse. Her teeth seemed a bit large for a person with such a small face, and that made her look all the more bright spirited as she talked with people next to her.

A shockwave went through him when he heard someone address her as Faith and he turned again to get a second look. He poured the coffee into his cup and waited for the woman to catch up to him.

"I hear you're the speaker tonight."

She looked up, stirring her coffee. "Yes, that's me. Faith," she said introducing herself.

He had heard it correctly. Close up the woman was attractive in an ordinary kind of way, her cropped dark hair beginning to go gray. She could not be *his* Faith, young and slim with long flowing hair, the woman he had imagined all year raising her white gown before stepping into the pool. It was all fantasy, he realized, but so what!

"I'm Will. Your name is Faith?"

"Yes," she said.

He decided to come right out with it. "Did you lose a personal diary sometime last year?"

Her jaw dropped. She put her hand to her mouth. As if on cue they both stepped aside to get away from people milling around.

"I wrote a diary," she said, "the year I got sober; and yes, I did lose it; but I thought I'd lost it in my house. I just expected that it would turn up one day."

"Well, Faith," he said, "I found your diary last December. You've been my anonymous sponsor ever since."

The stranger he knew so well now gripped his arm, and she used care to hold her hot coffee with the other hand.

"I use much of what I wrote in that diary in talks I prepare for engagements such as this. I had the diary in my briefcase when I met with a former colleague. Now, I work in Amherst. Long after that meeting, I looked for my diary but couldn't find it; I assumed it was misplaced somewhere in my house. Where did you find it?"

"I parked on a street near Union Station and I found it near the wheel of my car. I took it with me and put an ad in the newspaper. When no one claimed it, I started reading it. Maybe I should apologize for reading something that was so private, but the truth is . . . it helped me get through this year. I'd like to return it to you as soon as possible. I can come back here tomorrow?"

"I *would* like to have it back. I'm glad you found it helpful. We can meet here in the parking lot tomorrow, if that's okay with you. Say at seven? This is so unbelievable."

"Yes, it is." he replied. "I never expected to find you."

Will was trying to absorb the shock of seeing the woman who was so different from the picture in his head, so unlike the woman he had imagined who had helped him out of his darkest days of misery.

People settled into their chairs. A man at the podium was giving Faith the high sign that he was about to introduce her. Faith whispered, "I'll see you in the parking lot tomorrow at seven."

Will took his seat and soon the applause went up for Faith.

She introduced herself in the usual manner. "My name is Faith. I'm an alcoholic. I've been sober for fourteen years and I'm here tonight to share my experience, my strength, and my hope."

Fourteen years! His face flushed. *The diary was written fourteen years ago!* Random thoughts tumbled from Will's mind like an overturned bushel of pears, rendering him incapable of gathering his senses or regaining his composure. He tried to order the chaos in his mind and take hold of himself while simultaneously listening to what Faith was saying.

"When I made the decision to get sober," he heard her say, "I believed the hardest part was over by virtue of that decision, and that recovery would eventually come about in the AA rooms; all I had to do was sit and listen to people talk about their lives.

"My story is probably similar to yours. I would ask you to think back to how long it took to process the first three steps. It took me almost a year. I kept saying 'I already believe in a higher power so why not skip that step.'

"But, I was obstinate, trying to rely on my weak self instead of a higher power. Believing in or giving credence to a higher power isn't the most difficult part. It's *relying* on a higher power that's most difficult. *Relying* counts the most for people in recovery. Sure, we must have self respect, and we need strength to maintain that. But, here's the kicker," Faith went on. "Before we can rely on a higher power, we must allow something in us to die, so to speak. We must give up the idea of ourselves as all-powerful and build a new person inside. Many of us spin our wheels, struggling to stay sober while trying to hold onto the old image of ourselves; but that doesn't work. We must give up the image of ourselves as drinkers. The person lifting the glass must die. That image must be buried in a grave because that image cannot co-exist with staying sober.

"I'd like to read from my manuscript, the part about ego. This is a special kind of burial . . . burial of the ego that took so long to give in to a higher power.

"*My mind grieves for what I must give up. The life that I knew is over. The water is running free, dry leaves skate across the surface of the pond, little boats with their sails up. I am here for a burial and this death gives me hope. My inclinations have lost their vigor, and my habits are as useless as dried paramecium. This death goes without ceremony. No flowers, no cars, no people to bid farewell. Even the caretaker has gone home for the day. But for me, the faucets are flowing. Gravediggers arrive. Their shovels turn over the raw earth. My old habits kick up as stones. It's not easy to bury the ego. The gravediggers seem not to notice, so I keep one stone for myself, the gem set free in the thaw. They stop for a smoke and flick hot butts in my face. They survey their work and determine I will be theirs after the next round. When they're done they'll go off to dig another grave. They got what they came for. Grass will grow over this grave and give rest to the sheep.*"

When Faith finished speaking, the audience applauded. A few people gathered around her to ask questions. Will caught her eye before he left and gave her a thumbs-up to confirm their meeting the next evening. He went out to the parking lot behind St. Bridget's, still in a daze over their encounter. It was a wonder to him that a diary written fourteen years ago would reveal the struggle of today, but then he remembered that Bill Wilson's insights of the 1930s were still alive in every AA room.

The diary had become important to him, intrinsic, the way family, the Army, and architecture had become part of the fabric of his life, and now, Laura. He had taken the diary for granted, having had it so long at arm's length. Now he wondered how much of it he had absorbed and whether he could resume the journey without it. He thought of

Buffalo Boy having to remember the wisdom of Second Father because he couldn't read from the sacred book. He felt a sense of loss, wondering what his days would be like without being able to pick up Faith's diary from his night table.

CHAPTER 30

Market Street Café

The next evening, the nearly vacant parking lot at St. Bridget's indicated that no meetings were going on. Will arrived at 7:00 p.m. *There she is* he thought, seeing the only vehicle in the lot—a Volvo of all things. He pulled alongside the tan wagon and rolled down his car window.

"Looks like an all-Volvo parking lot," he said, making Faith laugh.

"I'll bet there's more mileage on mine than on yours," she quipped. "I was thinking—maybe we could go over to the Market Street Café, unless you're in a hurry."

"Good idea," Will replied. "I'll follow you."

That's more like it, he thought, driving behind her, trying to keep up. This was not just a matter of returning a book that was found. He wanted to spend time with her and get to know the person behind the story; the anonymous woman who had saved his life. It seemed odd now seeing the diary on the passenger seat where he had initially placed it on that fateful morning when he couldn't think of what else to do with it. He hadn't wanted to keep it, and those first days of having it in his possession had bothered him as much as something caught between his teeth. Faith's tale was fearsome, calling attention to inner demons that could topple the world if awakened. The words on those pages had brought Will to admit the truth—wanting to be sober but not wanting to give up drinking, having the tiger by its tail. Now he was troubled by the thought of returning a book that never belonged to him in the first place. When he arrived at the café Faith was just getting out of her car, and it occurred to him that she had driven like a man. It was no wonder that he had a hard time keeping up with her. He chuckled, knowing he would keep that to himself if he knew what was good for him. There she was, now, looking even more petit with the build of an adolescent boy, wiry and spare.

"Two-hundred and three thousand," she said right off about her mileage.

"You beat me by fifty thousand," he replied and in that instant their friendship was underway.

"I haven't been here in the evening," he said. "Looks busy."

"Good place to meet my friends. It's nice because they leave you alone to talk over a Cappuccino."

The waiter seated them and took their order.

"Decaf Cappuccino," Faith said, and then added with little hesitation, "and angel cake ala mode." She looked at Will, grinning like the Cheshire Cat. "Why not, this is a day to celebrate."

Will liked her. "Regular decaf, black," he said to the waiter.

"Glad we got a booth. We can talk without having to whisper," she remarked.

"By the way," Will said, "nice job last night. The part about the ego really moved people. I recognized it from your diary."

He removed the diary from his pocket and placed it on the table. Faith looked at it as if she were seeing it for the first time. She shook her head in disbelief and then opened it to the first page.

"My name is Faith," she read. "I'm an alcoholic."

Her dark brown eyes glistened, and for a moment her voice trailed off. "What a day that was," she said.

"Yeah," Will replied. "There's nothing more naked than that."

He reached out and pressed lightly on the back of her hand, and she smiled, their eyes saying, *I know what your road was like getting here.*

"Your diary had more of an impact on my recovery than anything," he was happy to tell her. "I'm sort of the quiet type . . . not for group stuff, if you know what I mean."

She smiled and nodded, letting him go on.

"I felt that your words spoke directly to me. Each page brought me closer to the truth. I became concerned about you. Now I see that you're okay."

"I'm doing fine," she replied. "I teach to earn a living but I speak in AA rooms to keep honest. The portion I read last night on the ego is right out of the diary, as you recognized. Fourteen years ago, that was a turning point for me.

"You say you have a long way to go. Where are you in your recovery?" she asked.

"I'm better now that I'm on anxiety medication. If it weren't for that, I'd be living each day on the brink of disaster," Will admitted. "Sometimes the urge to drink comes over me without much warning. It scares me to think that I can be that close to losing everything I value.

"Sometimes I long to let my mind go numb, the way I used to with alcohol. That's the remedy I discovered when I was a kid in the Army. I know how dangerous it is to let that desire go unchecked, but sometimes desire is stronger than the fear of consequences."

They exchanged tales about their life experiences and history of alcohol addiction. Faith advised him to use extreme care while taking anxiety medication. She admitted that she had been a virtual prisoner herself until she was able to face the truth about her addiction: that it was not something she could control and that she still needed help to keep sober.

"Some people have difficulty submitting to a higher power because they think it means giving up on their self control; abandoning reason. But, I have found the opposite to be true. Ego is what keeps us from seeing who we really are. If we allow ego to control us then who or what is in control? Underneath the façade of ego a better person exists and that's the one we must discover and nurture. That's the one who will save us. We save ourselves!"

"It's hard when the façade is what you relied on all your life," Will admitted.

"Ego is a façade and a necessary one to be sure," she added. "But even if that's what we present to the public, we must not be fools to ourselves by letting ego keep us from knowing our truth. No matter what we present to the outside world, we must always be aware of who we really are underneath the scrim of ego."

"Yes," Will said, understanding her fully. "I'm still struggling with that."

Faith revealed more about her struggle.

"Fourteen years ago, I believed that AA would perform miracles without much effort on my part and when that didn't happen, I realized that I had to do some work on myself. Maybe you're expecting AA to perform some kind of magic. Here's what I discovered. You must look hard at yourself. AA is not a mother and it's not for wimps. It's a path, a way, a support, a community of people who are addicted, and it's not in competition with anything. It offers wisdom derived from people's experiences; a place to meet and a community that supports you on the twelve-step path. You can take it or leave it. It's all up to you. The truth may seem harsh but anything but the truth will eventually do you in."

"I know what you're saying," Will replied. "It's just that I keep wavering, thinking I can beat it."

"You're still fighting the truth. People like us have to work the rest of our lives to keep the monkey off our backs. We're not like other people who can be casual about the cocktail hour. We cannot allow ourselves to be taken in by the attraction of happy hour or anything related to it. All that glamour with cigarettes and alcohol and glasses raised high telling us that life in the fast track will go on forever. That's the short-lived fantasy we must give up. Life for us is different. It becomes a series of daily choices.

"No more living by rote and letting habits reign, because our habits and inclinations will eventually bring us back to alcohol. Living must be thoughtful and regulated. Believe me, that style is not easy for someone like me who enjoys a casual lifestyle and doing things on the spur of the moment. Every decision I make must be a prudent one. Do I go to the social events that may be dangerous? No. If a friend invites me to dinner and serves alcohol, it's my responsibility to know whether that puts me in jeopardy, and if it does, then I must beg off. Friends of a certain type often go bye-bye when you don't drink with them. We have to learn to take care of ourselves. It's our life we're talking about. Go slack one day and you'll pay a big price."

"I hear you," Will said. "But doesn't all that regulation take the fun out of life?"

"You would think so, but it doesn't. The fun of life returns when you meet that other person inside you. If you can take that first step and patiently work through the process, eventually you'll become the person who wants to emerge. There's someone living inside your skin that wants to come out. Either you give him air and let him breathe or keep him dead. It's as simple as that."

When they agreed it was time to leave the café Faith reached for the check. "No, this is on me, I'm a big spender," Will said, jokingly.

The waiter thanked them and told them to stay as long as they wanted.

"I was thinking," Will said. "My head understands that I'm powerless but my gut won't accept it. I'm afraid to make that leap because it makes me feel like I'm giving up on myself. Like a small death."

"It *is* like a death," she said. "That's why I wrote about the death of the ego. I think what makes it so hard is that you have to say good-bye to that ego-driven person you're so used to, the one you know so well. You have to be willing to make the acquaintance with that stranger inside you and let him be. I'll never forget the day I knew there was someone else inside me. I was driving in my car and suddenly I felt an inner strength, as though I had at that moment become converted to someone I liked and respected. Nothing could defeat that sense of self. I discovered an inner strength when I found humility and accepted it as a way of being true to myself. So often, pride gets in the way. Arrogance may be the most difficult habit to break, the pride of the will. When you let it go, you'll find peace. If you're not there yet, you may be someday."

It was almost nine o'clock when they agreed for the second time to leave the café. Before leaving the booth they exchanged addresses and telephone numbers.

"I'd like to see you again?" she said.

"I was about to say the same," Will replied. "There's more I'd like to discuss with you. You're so far ahead of me in the process."

"Yes and no," she replied. "I am seasoned, that's true; and my Volvo has more mileage on it than yours. But we both begin each day with the same prayer. I'm focused now on speaking commitments and some writing so I keep myself very busy. You'll find that work will help to keep you structured. It's good that you're going back to your profession. There's nothing like it. Hard work is a good thing."

"Yeah," Will agreed. "Next week I'll be going back full time."

"I'd like to know more about your journey with the burden of anxiety . . . and if you would share your experience with me I could use the information to help others when I go on speaking engagements. You might even accompany me sometime. Would you be open to that?"

"I'd like to help. It's easier for me to talk about this now," he replied. "Your diary helped me, so maybe I can help you. Sure, let's meet again. Give me a call. If Laura answers . . . she's my fiancée, she'll know who you are. I told her about you last night."

"The air feels good," Faith said as they stood outside.

"The weather is changing over to a new season," Will said, reluctant to say good-bye.

But Faith surprised him when she took his hand. "I'd like you to take this with you and keep it for a while longer," she said, offering him the diary.

Will was reluctant to accept it, even though he wanted it back.

"It's okay, really," she said. "I'll know where it is if I need it. You have more work to do on yourself. If my diary helps you find that stranger inside you, then that's better than keeping it tucked away in my drawer."

"I'm grateful to you," he said, taking the diary from her hand.

"This is a good day for both of us, Will. Good luck with getting back to your profession," Faith remarked.

Will hugged her, and he felt that he could twice wrap his arms around the small body looking frail as a bird but made of steel. They'd be seeing each other again.

"Take good care of that Volvo," he called out. She waved to him and the overhead light in the parking lot reflected on her toothy smile.

She's real, he thought starting out slowly behind the tan Volvo, watching Faith maneuver her car into the flow of traffic with the moves of an Indy driver, and in seconds she was out of sight. The mystery is over, he realized, she's flesh and blood. He turned into the busy thoroughfare and headed for home. Laura would be waiting for him. He thought of Cozy and wondered if Laura would want a dog. Will's heart leapt.